"I couldn't have done it without you, Jo."

"You were doing all right before I came," she said quietly.

"Maybe, but I wouldn't have been able to keep working. It was impossible. I was almost at the end of my tether when you came along."

His touch was warm and his fingers strong as his hand covered hers.

"I'll always be grateful," he added.

Gratitude. Was that all it was? Was that all he felt toward her? What else could she expect? Nothing surely. Lewis was her employer, albeit for such a brief time—nothing more, nothing less. But she knew she would miss the intimacy that had grown between them. Knew without a shadow of a doubt that she would miss *him*.

Laura MacDonald lives in the United Kingdom, on the Isle of Wight. She is married and has a grown-up family. She has enjoyed writing fiction since she was a child, but for several years she worked for members of the medical profession, both in pharmacy and general practice. Her daughter is a nurse and has helped with the research for Laura's medical stories.

Holding the Baby
Laura MacDonald

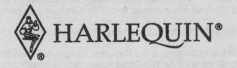

HARLEQUIN®

TORONTO • NEW YORK • LONDON
AMSTERDAM • PARIS • SYDNEY • HAMBURG
STOCKHOLM • ATHENS • TOKYO • MILAN • MADRID
PRAGUE • WARSAW • BUDAPEST • AUCKLAND

ISBN 0-373-51138-8

HOLDING THE BABY

First North American Publication 2001.

Copyright © 1999 by Laura MacDonald.

All rights reserved. Except for use in any review, the reproduction or utilization of this work in whole or in part in any form by any electronic, mechanical or other means, now known or hereafter invented, including xerography, photocopying and recording, or in any information storage or retrieval system, is forbidden without the written permission of the publisher, Harlequin Enterprises Limited, 225 Duncan Mill Road, Don Mills, Ontario, Canada M3B 3K9.

All characters in this book have no existence outside the imagination of the author and have no relation whatsoever to anyone bearing the same name or names. They are not even distantly inspired by any individual known or unknown to the author, and all incidents are pure invention.

This edition published by arrangement with Harlequin Books S.A.

® and TM are trademarks of the publisher. Trademarks indicated with ® are registered in the United States Patent and Trademark Office, the Canadian Trade Marks Office and in other countries.

Visit us at www.eHarlequin.com

Printed in U.S.A.

CHAPTER ONE

'SCALPEL. Scalpel— Are you with us, Nurse?'

'Oh, I'm so sorry.' Thankful for the mask that covered her reddened cheeks, Jo Henry took the scalpel from the tray of instruments in front of her and passed it to the surgeon, at the same time only too aware of the amused glances from the other members of the operating team.

She had been so concerned with making sure that the instruments were all in the correct order on the trolley that she had missed the surgeon's first request.

Still trying to cover her confusion, Jo glanced up from beneath her lashes only to meet the steady, solemn gaze of the anaesthetist as he sat beside the patient, carefully monitoring blood pressure and breathing. The man's gaze behind a pair of round, wire-framed spectacles was so direct as to be disconcerting and simply added to Jo's embarrassment. Hastily she looked down again and tried to concentrate on the operation.

The patient, the last on that morning's list for day surgery, was a young man in his thirties who was suffering from an inguinal hernia, which had been the direct result of heavy lifting on the building site where he was employed.

The surgeon completed the incision and took the diathermy machine from Jo to seal off the blood vessels. By this time the hernia was clearly visible, protruding through the layers of tissue, and as Jo and the rest of the team observed Mr Galloway, the surgeon, he manipulated the hernia back into place.

While the wound was being sutured Jo snipped each stitch then carefully checked swabs, needles and blades. When everything was complete she applied a dressing to the wound site then—while the anaesthetist checked the patient's condition and disconnected the anaesthetic tubes—Jo cleared away the instruments.

'Are you on after lunch, Jo?' asked Pru, the other duty staff nurse when they had almost finished clearing up.

'No.' Jo shook her head. 'I'm only on a part-time contract at the moment. It was all there was on offer when I applied here so I didn't have much choice. But I really will need to get more hours as soon as I can.'

'I don't think there'll be much else on this unit,' said Pru doubtfully.

'Then maybe I shall have to look elsewhere,' Jo replied. 'I trained as a nursery nurse before I did my RGN training so I may have to look in that direction.'

'What about accommodation?'

'Oh, yes, I'm fixed up there all right. I've got a small studio flat.'

'Well, that's something, I suppose,' said Pru.

'Thank you, ladies.' The anaesthetist had finished tidying his equipment and he stood up and nodded to the two staff nurses. He didn't smile and now that he had removed his cap and mask Jo could see that his hair was cut very close to his head and that the eyes behind the spectacles were an unusual sort of greyish-green.

'Is he always that solemn?' she asked as the anaesthetist left the theatre.

Pru nodded. 'Yes, he's a very quiet man.' She paused. 'But he's all right,' she added thoughtfully as she watched him go. Turning to Jo again, she asked curiously, 'So what brought you to Queensbury?'

'I used to visit here as a child,' Jo replied briefly. She left it there. She didn't want to go into details about how she had come to Queensbury after she had split up with Simon—how the whole thing had left her traumatised and vulnerable and how she had felt the overwhelming need for a fresh start.

After the two women had changed they made their way out of the day surgery unit and into the busy staff canteen.

'Have a cup of tea and a sandwich with me before you go,' said Pru.

Jo was about to refuse to say she had to get home,

then she shrugged and nodded. 'Yes, all right,' she said. 'That would be nice.' After all, what did she have to rush home for? What she needed now was to get to know people, to make new friends, and there was no doubt about it—Pru really had gone out of her way to be friendly and to show Jo the ropes.

'Well, hello, there. I haven't seen *you* before.'

Jo had become so lost in her thoughts she hadn't heard anyone approach the table where she'd sat down, daydreaming, while she waited for Pru to return with the drinks. She looked up with a start to find a dark-haired, very handsome young doctor smiling down at her.

'Hello,' she said. His smile was infectious and she found herself smiling back. 'No, you haven't seen me before,' she agreed, 'because I'm new here.'

'Well, that's the best news I've heard all day.' He laughed, revealing very white, even teeth. 'I'm pleased to meet you. The name's Jacobs, by the way. Marcus Jacobs.'

'Jo Henry,' she replied.

'So, tell me, Jo.' He sat down in one of the chairs, crossed one leg over the other and, folding his arms, began to scrutinise her with great interest. 'What department are you in?'

'Surgical day unit,' Jo replied, once again feeling the only too familiar tell-tale flush touching her cheeks. She hated herself for it and at the same time knew that he, too, had seen it. He really was incred-

ibly good-looking, with the darkest of eyes and the
sort of lashes that any girl would kill for. His air of
self-confidence, however, suggested that he was well
aware of the fact.

'Well, well, well,' he said softly. 'This gets better
and better. I'm Mr Hughes's houseman... Looks like
we could be working together.'

'Don't listen to him,' said Pru, setting a full tray
suddenly down on the table between them. 'He's
trouble.'

'How can you say such a thing? I'm mortified.'
Marcus Jacobs pressed one hand to his heart. He
spoke casually but for the most fleeting of moments
Jo had the impression that he was irritated by Pru's
intervention.

'Yes, I'll bet you are,' Pru went on acerbically.
'But it doesn't alter the fact that it happens to be
true. Jo is new here and anyone who is new needs
protection.'

'You're making me sound like some sort of mon-
ster who eats nurses for breakfast,' protested Marcus.

'Well?' Pru raised her eyebrows and Jo was forced
to laugh.

'I'm not!' He, too, laughed then, diffusing the
slight tension. Turning to Jo, he said, 'You'll have
to give me the chance to prove otherwise. Are you
coming to the Seventies night at the social club next
Saturday?'

'I don't know…' Jo glanced at Pru. 'Are you going?' she asked.

Pru nodded. 'Yes,' she said. 'We all are…'

'In that case, yes, I guess I am.' Jo nodded. When Marcus gave a wide smile she said, 'Only one small problem…'

'And what is that?' he said quickly.

'I'm not even a member of the club.'

'That's no problem.' Marcus stood up. 'Just leave it to me. I'll get you an application form.' He winked at Jo. 'See you girls. Enjoy your lunch.'

'Well, we might now,' said Pru as the houseman moved away.

'Is he really that bad?' asked Jo, staring after him as he left the canteen.

'He'll try it on with you,' said Pru as she bit into a sandwich. 'But that's pretty standard for Marcus. He tries it on with everyone, especially anyone who's new to the scene or who hasn't been warned of his reputation.'

'He's very good-looking…' said Jo.

'And he knows it,' said Pru pulling a face.

'Well, you needn't worry about me,' said Jo, taking a bite of her own sandwich. 'I'm not about to succumb to his charms, or to anyone else's for that matter.'

'Oh? Any particular reason?' Pru raised a speculative eyebrow.

'I'm off men at the moment,' said Jo lightly.

'Bad experience?' There was a touch of sympathy in Pru's voice now.

'I suppose you could say that.' Jo sighed. 'His name was Simon. He was young, good-looking, good prospects and he promised undying love…'

'And the crunch?'

'I wasn't the only one he'd promised it to.'

'Ah,' said Pru. 'So men really are off at the moment.'

Jo nodded, then, glancing up, said, 'How about you?'

'Me?' Pru looked faintly startled. 'Oh, I'm a walking disaster area in the romance stakes. I only have to give so much as one come-hither look and everything goes pear-shaped.'

'Sounds like we're pretty much two of a kind at the moment, then,' said Jo.

'Welcome to St Theresa's,' said Pru drily.

'Are you Joanne Henry?' Jo looked up as someone spoke behind her. A young nurse stood there.

'Yes,' Jo replied. 'That's me.'

'Mr Gregson said could he please have a word with you?'

'Mr Gregson?' Jo frowned. 'Who's Mr Gregson?'

It was Pru who answered. 'Lewis Gregson,' she replied. 'The anaesthetist.'

'Oh,' said Jo. 'Is that his name? I didn't know. Whatever does he want?'

'I don't know,' said the nurse. 'He just asked me

to give you the message. He's in the nurses' station but he said to finish your lunch first.'

'That's big of him.' Pru gave a short laugh.

'Whatever do you suppose he wants?' asked Jo anxiously as the nurse went away.

'Goodness knows,' said Pru as she swallowed her tea.

'Do you think I was doing it all wrong this morning?' said Jo. 'Is that what he wants, to tell me off?'

'Shouldn't think so. It certainly didn't look to me as if you were doing anything wrong.' Pru stood up and, looking down at Jo, went on, 'Besides, even if you had done something wrong, it's not for him to tell you. He'd have to take it up with our manager, Miss Allford. Anyway, I shouldn't worry about it. Just go and see what he wants. He can't eat you.' She glanced at her fob watch. 'I must fly—I'm back in Theatre in ten minutes. I'll see you tomorrow, Jo.'

'Yes, all right, Pru. See you. Oh, and thanks for lunch.'

'That's OK.' Pru flashed her friendly smile and was gone, out of the canteen and back to the day unit, leaving Jo still sitting at the table wondering what on earth it could be that the poker-faced Lewis Gregson wanted to see her about.

She went to the ladies first—just to freshen up, she told herself. But if she was really truthful it was to check her appearance, to comb her short blonde hair and to apply a touch of lipstick—more as a boost to

her confidence than anything else because, in spite
of Pru's reassurances to the contrary, she was still
apprehensive over why the anaesthetist should want
to see her.

Had she been at fault in the procedures in the theatre? she wondered as she studied her reflection in
the mirror. It had been some little while since she'd
worked as a scrub nurse in Theatre, her last post
having been on an orthopaedic ward, but she hadn't
thought she'd seemed too rusty. Maybe she was
wrong.

With a little sigh she replaced her make-up in her
bag, smoothed down her long skirt and slipped on
her jacket. She felt ready now to face whatever it
might be she had to face and, taking a deep breath,
she made her way out to the nurses' station.

True to his word Lewis Gregson was sitting behind
the main desk, talking to Julian Browne, the charge
nurse on duty. As she approached both men looked
up.

'Ah, here she is,' said Julian, as if they had been
discussing her. 'Use my office if you like, Lewis.
You won't be disturbed in there.'

'Thanks, Julian.' Lewis Gregson got to his feet and
nodded to Jo. 'Thanks,' he said briefly, before leading the way into the charge nurse's office. He held
the door open for her then closed it firmly behind
both of them.

There were only two chairs in the office, one behind the large desk and one facing it. He indicated for Jo to take the chair facing the desk while he took the other. It felt formal, like an interview, and only added to Jo's sense of apprehension.

'I expect you are wondering what I want to see you about,' he said calmly. Dressed in a charcoal grey suit with a faint pinstripe, a crisp white shirt and a plain tie, he looked cool, utterly in control and every inch the successful consultant anaesthetist.

'Well, yes. I am, as a matter of fact,' Jo agreed. 'Is it something to do with my work?' she said at last. 'I haven't actually been working in Theatre for some time but I'm sure in time—'

'What?'

She looked up quickly, miserably almost, only to find that he was staring at her in amazement.

'Well, isn't that what this is about…my work…?' She trailed off.

'No.' He answered sharply. 'Good Lord, no. Absolutely not. Nothing like that at all. I say, I'm sorry if you thought…'

'Then what…?' She frowned. 'I don't understand.' She couldn't imagine what else he might want to see her about. She didn't even know the man, hadn't really even been properly introduced, had only seen him in Theatre. And he was clearly disturbed that she had thought he might be about to reprimand her.

'I wanted to ask you something,' he said. 'You

see, I overheard you talking in Theatre. I heard you say you wanted more hours.'

'Well, yes, that's true. I do.' Jo nodded, wondering what on earth he was going to suggest.

'You said that you'd trained as a nursery nurse.'

'That's right. That was before I started my RGN training.'

'So you like children?'

'Oh, yes, I do. I like children.'

'And have you had any experience of actually working with children?'

'Not a great deal,' Jo admitted. 'I had one job, looking after two young children, after I'd completed my training. It was when that family moved to the States that I decided to go for my RGN.'

'I see. Well, I was wondering...' He paused briefly, while maintaining his steady gaze. 'Would you be interested in a part-time position, looking after three children?'

'Three children?' She stared at him. She hadn't taken him for a family man.

'Yes.' He nodded. 'Three quite young children, as it happens. It would only be temporarily and it could be tailored to fit in with your hours here.' He was watching her closely now, his expression inscrutable.

'What exactly would this entail?' she asked, leaning forward slightly in her chair.

'Well...' He took off his spectacles and began polishing them with a spotlessly white handkerchief. 'I would want you to live in.'

'Live in?' She looked up sharply.

'Yes, because there are things I'm finding it difficult to keep track of.' He took a deep breath and put the polished spectacles not back on his nose, as Jo had expected him to do, but in the top pocket of his jacket. 'There are so many things that their mother did each day, things like packing lunch boxes, organising games kit, visits to the clinic—you know the sort of thing, I'm sure—things which, I'm afraid, I'm simply not familiar with.'

He spread his hands and suddenly Jo felt a stab of pity for him. It was obvious he had been widowed or that his wife had left him.

'Like I say,' he went on, while Jo was still struggling for something to say, 'it is only a temporary post, just while the children's mother is abroad.'

So that ruled out the widower theory. 'And do you know how long that is likely to be for?' asked Jo tentatively.

'Not at the moment. You see, it all depends… They are very nice children,' he added, his level gaze meeting hers again. 'And they really aren't that much trouble. It's just that…'

'They are obviously missing their mother very much,' Jo finished the sentence for him.

'Yes,' he agreed. He looked surprised that she

should make what was such a very accurate observation. 'Yes, they are.'

'So, how old are they—the children?' Jo prompted when he fell silent again.

'Well, Alistair, the eldest, is six.' He spoke almost as if he had difficulty remembering. 'Francesca is four and the baby, Jamie, is...six months. Yes, that's right, six months.'

'A baby?' said Jo faintly.

'Would that be a problem?' He frowned.

'Well, no, not really.' She gave a helpless little shrug, wondering how any woman in her right mind could leave a six-month-old baby. 'I don't suppose it would. Er, don't you have any other help at all?'

'There is a lady who comes in to clean twice a week and the child-minder who looks after Jamie while I'm at work. She also collects Alistair from school and Francesca from her nursery school each day, but I don't think she's prepared to do that for much longer. A neighbour is also helping out but, again, I don't know how long I can impose on her good nature. I took some annual leave last week,' he added, 'but I can't keep on doing that.'

'You said this position would only be a temporary one,' said Jo, mystified now as to what would happen in the future.

'Oh, yes,' he replied quickly. 'It's only until their mother returns.'

So she'd been wrong on both counts, Jo thought.

Not only was he not a widower but neither did it sound as if his wife had actually left him.

'Look,' he said briskly. 'Don't decide straight away. Come and see what's involved first.'

'Yes,' she said. 'That might be a good idea.'

'Could you come this evening?' he said. 'Damn!' he muttered as his pager suddenly went off. 'I shall have to go. Could you…?' he looked so confident that Jo found herself quite unable to refuse.

'What's the address?' she asked, taking a pen and a scrap of paper from her handbag.

'Forty-eight Mowbery Avenue,' he said. 'And the name of the house is Chilterns.'

'What time would you like me to come?'

'Would eightish be OK?' When she nodded, he went on, 'Hopefully, by then I should have the children in bed… I say, hopefully.' He smiled and, devoid of the studious-looking spectacles, it was a surprisingly boyish smile. 'Do you have transport?' he added as she stood up to go.

'Yes,' Jo replied. 'I have my car.'

'Good.' He nodded. 'I'll see you at eight, then.'

He looked different now, happier somehow than when she'd first come into the room. But by the time Jo had left the building and unlocked her car she was feeling rather less than happy herself. In fact, she was beginning to wonder what in the world had possessed her to agree to go to his house that evening.

It was true she was looking for more working

hours but ideally those hours would have been doing more of what she was already doing. What Lewis Gregson was proposing sounded quite horrendous and the more she thought about it the more she came to realise she really didn't want to do it.

She didn't want to move out of her new studio flat, even if it was only for a short length of time, and what guarantee did she have about that, anyway? She didn't know why his wife had chosen to go abroad and leave him with their three children. What if his wife decided she liked it wherever it was she'd gone, liked it better than 48 Mowbery Avenue with her husband and children—liked it so much that she decided not to return?

By then she, Jo, might have become attached to the children, or they to her, and she might find it difficult to extricate herself from the situation.

The hours and duties sounded as if they could be a bit of a nightmare as well. Little things, he'd said, like lunch boxes and trips to the clinic, but if Jo knew anything about it, that would no doubt extend to things like mountains of washing and ironing, supervising homework and tending to a fractious baby in the middle of the night. And as if all that wasn't enough, it was also on top of her everyday job on the day unit.

By the time she reached her flat, which was tucked away in a mews terrace on the edge of the Surrey town of Queensbury, Jo had come to a decision. She would phone Lewis Gregson and tell him she was very sorry but she really didn't think she could contemplate the job he had offered because it quite simply wasn't practical.

It was quiet and peaceful in her flat with its large, south-facing windows that caught the afternoon sunshine and her window-boxes packed with pansies and polyanthus. She couldn't imagine leaving here, even for a short time. It really was unthinkable, especially after the struggle she'd had in finding somewhere in the first place, somewhere she could call her own, somewhere she could retreat to to lick her wounds after Simon.

Sinking down onto her sofa, she kicked off her shoes.

There was a whole column of Gregsons in the telephone directory, but not one who lived in Mowbery Avenue.

Maybe, she thought, if she rang the hospital he might still be there and she could leave a message.

After dialling the number, she asked the girl on the switchboard to put her through to the day unit where she was informed that Mr Gregson had just left. She then asked to be put through to Personnel where she asked if it was possible to have Mr Gregson's phone number, only to be told that it was the policy of the hospital that staff details were never disclosed without the permission of the person involved.

In the end she gave up and resigned herself to the fact that she would have to go to his house as arranged, but at the same time she would have to make it absolutely plain to him that she now had no intention of taking up his offer.

CHAPTER TWO

SITUATED in a quiet avenue of cherry trees, the house was one of those rambling, three-storey, red-brick buildings of the Edwardian era.

Quite consistent with the salary of a consultant anaesthetist, thought Jo as she parked her rather elderly Metro outside and sat for a moment, looking up at the house.

It was almost dusk and the streetlights had just come on. It had rained around teatime, heavy showers which had drenched lawns and left large puddles in the gutters. Jo got out of her car, locked the door behind her and approached the house, her shoes making a crunching noise on the loose gravel.

There were three vehicles parked on the drive, two alongside each other to one side of the house. One of these was a large Range Rover and the other a smaller, red saloon. One was parked right in front of the door, this a small but expensive-looking, silver sports car.

Jo was just wondering to whom they all belonged when a security light above the front door suddenly came on and made her jump. She hesitated for a moment then stepped forward and rang the doorbell.

The door was opened almost immediately and Lewis Gregson stood there on the threshold, one finger pressed to his lips and a sleeping baby tucked into the crook of his arm.

'Shh,' he whispered. 'I've only just got him off.'

'Sorry,' Jo whispered back.

'Come in,' he said in the same hushed tones.

'Look, if it's not convenient...'

'No, no,' he said. 'I'm glad you've come. Please, come in.' He stood back, holding the door open with his free hand while Jo stepped into a spacious hallway.

'The other two are in bed,' he said as he closed the door behind her. 'Whether or not they are asleep is another matter. We've had *Postman Pat* three times and *Thomas the Tank Engine*, two cups of water and three trips to the loo...so, hopefully, I would think we're just about running out of excuses not to go to sleep.'

She wanted to tell him then, before he went any further, tell him she had only come to say she couldn't even consider what he had proposed—that it simply wouldn't work.

Instead, she found herself following him across the black-and-white-tiled floor of the hall and into a large, high-ceilinged sitting room. She stood for a moment on the threshold, looking around at the deep, comfortable-looking sofas, the beige, thick-piled carpet and the glass-topped coffee-tables, all of which were littered with a colourful assortment of children's toys and books.

'Sorry about the mess,' he said. 'I haven't had a chance to clear up yet.'

'That's OK,' Jo heard herself say. 'It must be very difficult for you.'

He looked different this evening. For a start he wasn't wearing his glasses, which led Jo to suspect he only wore them for close work. He was also casually dressed, in jeans and a sweatshirt, and somehow he looked younger than he did at work, without the formal business suit or the theatre greens.

Jo swallowed and steeled herself. She mustn't start feeling sorry for him—that wouldn't do her any good at all.

'Well, where shall we start?' he said, but before Jo had the chance to even open her mouth he went on, 'Maybe first you'd like to see over the house, just so you get some idea of the layout.'

'Actually…' Jo took a deep breath. 'Actually, I was thinking…' But that was as far as she got for at that moment the baby opened his eyes and began to whimper.

'Oh, no.' Lewis Gregson gave a deep sigh and stared down at the baby. 'Not again. I was just going to put you down in your cot, young man. I thought we'd heard the last of you for this evening.'

With that the baby's face crumpled and he let out a wail of rage and struggled to sit up. And as if that wasn't enough, a phone began ringing somewhere else in the house.

'Damn!' muttered Lewis under his breath. Looking at Jo, he said, 'Would you mind taking him for a moment while I answer that? It's probably his mother, ringing to make sure that everything is all right.'

He almost thrust the baby at her, giving her no option but to take him. Then he was gone out of the room, shutting the door firmly behind him and leaving Jo to try to pacify the wailing baby whose face by this time had turned brick-red and who was holding his breath between yells.

'Oh, come on, little one, there's no need for that.' Holding the baby upright, Jo leaned him slightly over her shoulder then, patting his back in an attempt to console him, she began walking around the large room.

Very gradually the baby's wails subsided, to be replaced by intermittent sobbing hiccups.

'There, there,' Jo soothed. 'That's better, isn't it, Jamie?'

By the time Lewis Gregson returned to the room some considerable time later the baby was dozing on Jo's shoulder.

'You must have a magic touch,' said Lewis Gregson admiringly. 'He's practically asleep. I suppose you wouldn't mind carrying him up to the nursery and putting him down in his cot, would you? If I take him from you, he'll probably start up again.'

'Er…yes, all right,' said Jo. She was beginning to think this whole thing was starting to spin out of her control. Lewis Gregson seemed to be under the misapprehension that it was a foregone conclusion that she would be taking up the position he had offered her. She would have to put him straight on that. Just as soon as she'd put the baby into his cot.

Silently she followed him out of the sitting room and up the stairs. The baby had cuddled right into her neck and shoulder by this time and was fast asleep. Glancing down, she saw dark lashes spiked against a flushed cheek and hair that curled damply around the creases of his neck while one hand clutched at her shirt. He smelt of baby powder and warm milk.

A dim light burned on the landing and two of the bedroom doors stood ajar. Lewis Gregson led the way down a short passage to a third room and pushed open the door.

Another subdued light burned in this room which quite obviously was a nursery. Against one wall was a cot, with a mobile of rabbits and pink elephants gently rotating above it. An alphabet frieze adorned the walls, together with several posters of Disney characters, while against a second wall the top of a white chest of drawers was littered with all the paraphernalia associated with the care of a young baby.

Jo crossed to the cot and as Lewis Gregson held back the covers she very carefully lowered the baby. She laid him on his back and held her breath for a moment as he stirred again, whimpered in his sleep, then gave a long, drawn-out sigh, before turning his head to one side.

Gently she drew up the covers and tucked them in firmly on either side of the mattress. Then she stood for a moment and gazed down at the sleeping baby, before looking across the cot at Lewis Gregson.

'Thanks,' he said simply.

'That's OK,' she replied. 'With a bit of luck he should sleep through now.'

'I can see,' he said as they tiptoed from the room, 'that I've done the right thing, asking you to come here.'

'Ah…' she said. 'I need to talk to you about that…'

'I was going to approach an employment agency,' he went on in the same low tones as they stood on the landing, 'but I couldn't entertain the idea of leaving them with a stranger.'

'But I'm a stranger. You hardly know me, and the children don't know me at all,' Jo protested.

'True,' he admitted, 'but I know you from working with you, even if it has only been for a short time. I know the children will like you—see how Jamie responded to you—and I also know you came to the hospital with good references. I took the liberty of checking with Julian Browne. Let's face it, you can't be too careful these days where young children are concerned.'

'No,' she said faintly. 'I suppose not...'

'Another thing that would prove difficult in employing someone from an agency, or through an advertisement, is the fact that this is only a temporary position.' He paused. 'And, of course, that would suit you as well because, as you said, you are only waiting for something else to come up at the hospital, which it will before too long.'

'Mr. Gregson.' She took a deep breath.

'Lewis, please. Call me Lewis,' he said quickly.

He really did have nice eyes, she thought, especially when he allowed himself that rare smile. 'Right, Lewis,' she said. 'Well, I do need to talk to you about all this.'

He stared at her for a moment. 'Of course you do. I'm sorry, I should have thought. You'll want to know about things like pay and conditions—'

'Actually, I really wanted to—'

'We'll go downstairs and talk, but first...take a look in here.'

Before she could stop him he had moved down the landing and gently pushed open one of the doors that stood ajar.

'This is Francesca's room,' he whispered.

Peering inside, Jo's eyes gradually became adjusted to the gloom and in the light from the landing she could just see the shape of a small child beneath the covers on the bed. A tangle of dark curls were spread across the pillow while one arm was flung across a rag doll that lay beside the little girl.

'And this,' he went on rapidly, pulling the door again, moving to the second room and pushing its door open, 'is Alistair's room.'

All that Jo could see in here was a mound in the bed, one small pyjama-clad bottom stuck into the air and tousled head burrowed into the pillow.

'Mr Gregson—Lewis,' she whispered urgently, 'please, please, can we talk?'

'Yes, of course. Come on, we'll go down and hope we get a bit of peace and quiet for a while.'

She followed him down the stairs and this time, instead of leading the way into the sitting room, he headed down a passage to the rear of the hall and opened a door which led into the kitchen.

Like all the other rooms it was large, its walls covered with stripped pine shelves and cupboards. An Aga took up one wall, an old-fashioned dresser another, and in the centre, on the quarry-tiled floor, stood an old, farmhouse-style table and chairs.

A baby's high chair was placed at one end of the table and on a line strung across the Aga was a selection of children's clothing—socks, underclothes, Babygros, pyjamas, shirts and blouses.

'It's a problem, getting it all ready,' Lewis said,

following her gaze. 'They seem to get through so much.'

'Don't you have a tumble-drier?' Jo asked, looking around.

'Oh, yes,' he replied, 'and an automatic washing machine. But it's the airing—I can never convince myself everything is aired. God knows how Becky gets it all done.'

So that was his wife's name. Becky.

'She works part time as well. She designs and markets her own greeting cards. Her studio and office are on the top floor.'

One of those superwomen who could do everything with one arm tied behind their backs, thought Jo. Once again she wondered where Becky had gone. Maybe it was something to do with this business of hers. Whatever it was, it still seemed a bit unfair to land Lewis with everything. On the other hand, maybe the woman was simply trying to prove some sort of point.

'Can I get you a drink?' asked Lewis suddenly, as if the thought had only just occurred to him. 'What would you like? Tea, coffee or something a little stronger?'

'A cup of tea would be nice,' Jo heard herself say. She didn't know why she said it because all she really wanted was to tell Lewis Gregson what she had come to say, then to hightail it out of this house with all its problems and get back to the comparative sanctuary of her flat.

'Right,' Lewis was saying, 'I'll just make a bit of space here.'

The table was littered with the remains of the evening meal, which looked as if it had been some sort of chicken dish, salad and jacket potatoes. There were also packets of baby cereal, rusks, jars of baby food and a row of dirty feeding bottles. 'I must get those washed and into the steriliser,' Lewis said as he realised Jo was looking at them.

'But...' he looked round '...first things first. Kettle.' Crossing to the sink, he filled the kettle then plugged it in and switched on the power. Opening one of the cupboards, he took out two mugs, and lifted down a cockerel-shaped teapot. From a tin he produced a couple of teabags and from the fridge a carton of milk.

'Sugar?' he said.

'No,' she replied. 'I don't.'

'There were some biscuits around here somewhere...' he said vaguely, as he waited for the kettle to boil.

'Oh, don't worry—please,' she said hastily.

'I think Alistair must have eaten them all,' he said with a shrug. 'Sorry...'

'Honestly, it doesn't matter...'

But he wasn't listening. Instead, he'd moved to a huge cork noticeboard on the far wall and was staring at one of the dozens of scraps of paper pinned to it with brightly coloured drawing-pins. 'I almost forgot,' he muttered, half to Jo, and half to himself, 'Alistair has got football practice tomorrow and Francesca has her ballet class.'

Running one hand over his closely cropped hair, he glanced over his shoulder at Jo. 'Those are the sort of things that I shall be grateful for your help with,' he said. 'As it is, I guess I'll have to try and finish work early again or impose on Sue even more.'

'Sue?' said Jo.

He nodded. 'The child-minder.' He paused as the kettle boiled and he poured the water into the teapot. 'She's been tremendous. I don't know what I would have done without her. But everyone has their limit, and I'm afraid if I pile too much onto her she'll just…' He shrugged, leaving the sentence unfinished.

'How do you cope in the mornings?' asked Jo. Suddenly she was curious. She knew he would have to be on the day unit by eight-thirty and she couldn't see how that could fit in with the household routine. 'Does the child-minder come here?'

'Heavens, no,' he said. 'I wish she did. That would make life much easier. No, I have to give the children their breakfasts.'

'Surely they don't start school until after you have to be at work?'

'Exactly,' he said. 'Jamie goes to the child-minder and she's agreed to let me drop the other two off there as well. She then very kindly runs them to school.'

'So what time do you have to get up?' Jo asked as she took the mug of tea he handed to her.

'Well, this morning it was five-thirty,' he said. 'But that was mainly because Jamie woke up early and I thought I might as well just get up as there didn't seem much point in going back to bed.'

'You really do need some help, don't you?' As she took a sip of her tea she allowed her gaze to meet his across the table.

'You could say that.' He paused, the greenish-grey eyes meeting hers. 'When can you start?'

'Lewis.' Setting her mug down, she took a deep breath. 'I haven't agreed to—'

'Oh, but you will. Won't you?' he said and there was a sudden flash of alarm in his eyes now, as if for the first time the possibility seemed to hit him that she might refuse.

'I'm not really sure…' she began slowly.

'All this has put you off, hasn't it?' He waved his hand at the mess on the table, the airing clothes and the dirty dishes stacked on the worktop.

'No…no, not really. It isn't that…'

'Then what? We haven't talked about pay yet. Is it that?'

'No, please, it isn't that either.' She paused. 'It's just that I'm not sure it's what I want. It's a lot to take on, you have to admit that. There's a lot of responsibility in looking after three children, especially three such young children…'

'Yes, I do know that,' he said. 'But you wouldn't be entirely on your own—I shall be here most of the time. The only time you would really be on your own with them would be when you pick Alistair and Francesca up at three o'clock, then Jamie from the child-minder. I can be home by five-thirty, six at the latest.'

'So, really, all you want is for someone to be here from three until six?' she asked as she began wondering if perhaps they could rethink this whole thing.

'No,' he said. 'I need someone here during the evening and at night in case I get called in to the hospital.'

'Oh, yes, of course,' she said. 'I'd forgotten that.'

'The other aspect, of course,' he went on, not giving her a chance to voice any more doubts, 'is that, hopefully, it will only be for a short time.'

'So just how long are we actually talking about?' she said at last.

'Just until their mother gets back.'

'Where is she exactly?'

'Africa.'

'Africa!' She stared at him in astonishment. It was the last thing she had expected him to say.

'Yes, Nairobi to be exact. The problem is we don't really have any idea just how long the situation will go on for. She just had to drop everything and go when it happened.'

'I'm sorry. I don't understand.' Jo looked bewildered. 'When what happened?'

'Didn't I say?' He looked amazed. 'Didn't I tell you what all this was about?'

'No,' she replied, trying to remain patient. 'No, you didn't.'

'I'm sorry. I thought I had—I certainly meant to. So, tell me, what do you know?'

'Simply that your wife has gone off and left you with the children—'

'My wife?' He was staring at her now.

'Yes.'

'Rebecca isn't my wife,' he said. 'I'm not married.'

'Really?' she said coolly. When she remained silent after that he threw her a sharp glance.

'The children aren't mine either. Is that what you thought?' He hit his forehead with the heel of his hand. 'I guess I'd better explain.'

'Yes,' said Jo faintly. 'I guess you had.'

'Rebecca, the children's mother, is my sister,' said Lewis. 'Her husband, David, is an engineer. He's been working on a water project in Nairobi for his company and he's been taken ill with some sort of amoebic dysentery. He is very seriously ill and can't be moved for the time being. Rebecca has flown out to be with him...'

'And left the children with you?'

'There was no one else,' he said simply. 'And I certainly wasn't having them go into care. Initially it was only for a few days. I took some annual leave and there wasn't too much of a problem. Then Rebecca phoned to say David had taken a turn for the worse. She didn't know what to do. I could tell she was torn between returning to the children or staying at David's bedside in case anything happened to him.'

'I see,' Jo said slowly. Suddenly there was a whole new slant on the situation. 'So what did you say to her?'

'I told her to stay with David,' he said simply. 'I knew really that was what she wanted but she was afraid I wouldn't be able to cope. She suggested I contact Sue to help with Jamie. Sue had minded the other two from time to time before Jamie was born so she was already well known to the family. Becky also said to get any other help I thought necessary. That's why I asked you,' he added with a shrug.

'So this isn't your home?' she said, looking around the large kitchen.

'Good grief, no.' He looked faintly startled. 'Is that what you thought? No, I have a very modest abode by comparison. I simply moved in here because it was easier, that's all. All the children's things are here and I didn't want to disrupt their lives any more than was necessary. Besides, I doubt they'd all fit in my apartment.'

'Was that your sister on the phone just now?'

'Yes, it was.' He nodded, but his expression had become grim.

'How is her husband?'

'He's hovering between life and death,' he replied. 'Apparently they are going to start a new treatment in the next few days—some drug that is being flown out there from this country. The whole thing is being organised by the company David works for—it seems they can't do enough—but the problem is he is so weak that it's doubtful his system will be able to tolerate the drug.'

'And in the meantime you have been literally left holding the baby?'

'You could say that.' Again he passed his hand over his hair. 'But there was never any question of it being otherwise. Becky and I have always looked out for each other. Our parents both died when we were quite young...so I guess that's just the way it's always been... Besides, Alistair is my godson... and...'

He paused and looked round the kitchen again, this time as if he were seeing the chaos for the first time. 'You've had second thoughts, though, haven't you? Actually, I can't say that I blame you. Couldn't really expect anyone to take this lot on...'

'When would you like me to start?' said Jo quietly.

'I mean, it's not exactly your usual run-of-the mill, part-time job, is it?' He carried on as if he hadn't heard her, then suddenly he stopped and, turning his head, stared at her. 'What did you say?' he said at last.

'I asked when you would like me to start?'

'I thought I must have misheard you,' he said. 'Well?'

'How about yesterday?' he said.

'OK. You're on,' she replied, trying to sound casual, as if this were the kind of thing she agreed to all the time. Then, before she had time to think what was happening, Lewis flung his arms around her, lifted her off the ground and whirled her round. Then, setting her down, he planted a kiss firmly on her mouth.

'You are wonderful,' he said. 'Has no one ever told you that?'

'Is that your girlfriend, Uncle Lew?' said a small, incredulous voice from the doorway.

Jo spun round to find a boy standing there. A small boy, rubbing the sleep from his eyes, his fair hair sticking up all over his head.

'No, Alistair,' said Lewis, trying to suppress the laughter in his voice. 'This is Miss Henry. She's going to help me look after you and Francesca and Jamie while your mum is away.'

'I thought she was your girlfriend,' said Alistair.

'No,' said Lewis again, 'she isn't my girlfriend.'

'Well,' said Alistair solemnly, 'if she isn't your girlfriend, you shouldn't really have been kissing her.'

CHAPTER THREE

'HE WANTS you to do what?' Pru stared at Jo in a sort of fascinated horror.

It was the following morning and the two of them were on the day unit, scrubbing up in readiness for the first of the patients for that day's surgery.

'To help him look after his sister's children while she's away,' Jo repeated patiently.

'But you say he wants you to move in?'

'Yes.' Jo nodded. 'Actually, that will make things easier. You see, he has to have someone there all the time in case he gets called in here for an emergency.'

'Sounds like a lot of hard work to me,' said Pru, pulling a face. 'Three children, did you say?' When Jo nodded she gave a little shudder. 'Well, rather you than me, that's all I can say.'

'It may not be as bad as it sounds. The baby goes to a child-minder during the day, the eldest is at school and the middle one, the little girl, is at nursery school.'

'How old is this baby exactly?'

'Six months.'

'Six months! Oh, for goodness' sake, Jo.' Pru looked at her aghast. 'It's probably teething. You'll have the most horrendous nights.'

'Well, I guess that's a chance I'll just have to take.' Jo gave a little shrug. Already she was beginning to wonder if the effects of her noble, selfless gesture weren't beginning to wear off a bit.

Pru was silent for a moment then she said, 'Talking of nights—is it just going to be you and him in that house on your own?'

'Not quite.' Jo gave a short laugh. 'There will be three children, in case you've forgotten.'

'Yes, yes, I know that,' said Pru impatiently. 'But you know what I mean. Thing is, the staff here will have a field day when they find out. You know how they love to gossip.'

'That's the least of my worries,' said Jo smartly.

'So you don't worry about what people might say?'

'No, I don't. I've never worried about things like that.'

'And it doesn't worry you that you'll be living in such close proximity to him—Lewis Gregson?'

'No. Why should it? He'll simply be my employer, that's all. Besides...' She paused.

'Besides what?' said Pru curiously.

'He isn't my type,' said Jo.

'Isn't he?' Pru screwed up her face, as if reflecting. 'Actually, I think he's rather nice. Quiet, of course, and a bit serious, but underneath all that I think he could be quite hunky.'

'Yes, well, maybe, but I won't be getting into any-

thing like that, I can assure you,' said Jo. 'And, anyway, I'm off men at the moment.'

'Would that include Marcus Jacobs, by any
chance?' Pru grinned, flashing Jo a sideways glance.

'What do you mean?' said Jo indignantly.

'Well, from the look on your face yesterday when
you were gazing up at him I wouldn't have said you
would be off him given half the chance.'

'Don't be silly,' said Jo, feeling a tell-tale flush
creeping into her cheeks.

'Oh,' said Pru as she turned from the line of washbasins, 'Talk of the devil. Looks like our resident
heart-throb is assisting Mr Hughes this morning.'

'Oh?' said Jo. Turning quickly, she was in time to
see the surgeon, Mr Hughes, and Marcus Jacobs enter the scrub room.

'Good morning, ladies.' Mr Hughes, a tall, grey-
haired, distinguished-looking man in his sixties, nodded at the two nurses.

While the girls murmured their greetings Marcus
caught Jo's gaze and winked at her. She smiled back
at him then, leaving the two men to scrub up, she
and Pru made their way into a small anteroom where
they donned green gowns over the trousers, tunics
and clogs they already wore. After securing their
masks, they made their way into Theatre where an
ODA—operating department assistant—informed
them that the patient was anaesthetised.

While Jo checked the patient details and confirmed

that the consent form had been duly signed, Pru made her way into the adjoining theatre where a gynae list was ready to proceed. As Jo was checking her trolly to make sure she had all the equipment that might be needed, the double doors from the anaesthetic room swung open and the patient was wheeled into Theatre.

She felt her gaze automatically drawn to the eyes above the mask as the anaesthetist took his place at the patient's head and began to check his own drugs and equipment. This morning those greenish-grey eyes were once again behind spectacle lenses but the gaze that met hers was as steady as ever.

'Hello, Jo,' he said quietly.

'Good morning, Mr Gregson,' she replied politely, correctly, mindful of his status in this room, which was equal to that of the surgeon. 'May I prepare Mrs Hewitt, please?'

Lewis checked the monitor, the oxygen and the patient's airway then nodded. 'Yes, she's fine,' he replied with a nod.

'Thank you,' Jo replied, then suddenly, almost uncomfortably aware of Lewis Gregson's continuing gaze upon her she began to prepare the patient's left leg with antiseptic solution in readiness for ligation and stripping of the saphenous vein.

When she had finished an ODA applied a tourniquet to the thigh which was duly inflated to cut off the blood supply. By the time Mr Hughes and

Marcus Jacobs entered the theatre in their greens and masks Jo had covered the patient with the appropriate green drapes.

'Good morning, everyone,' Mr Hughes peered over the top of his mask. 'Now, who do we have first?'

'This is Beryl Hewitt,' Jo replied.

'Yes, yes, of course.' Mr Hughes nodded. Half turning towards Marcus, his houseman, he said, 'This lady presented with dilated and tortuous veins, acute discomfort and oedema. Latterly there was also a degree of eczema and ulceration. I decided ligation and stripping was our only real option.' He turned to Lewis. 'Are we ready, Lewis?'

'Yes, Edward, absolutely,' Lewis replied.

'In that case,' said Edward Hughes with a glance round at his team, 'scalpel, please, Nurse.'

The incision was duly made in the patient's groin. Using wire, the saphenous vein was stripped then removed. When the operation was completed the veins were tied off, the skin sutured and dressings and bandages applied before the patient was taken into Recovery.

It proved to be a long morning with a varied list, but for Jo it was tiring because of the degree of concentration she needed, being so new to the job. She also felt she was the object of some scrutiny. To a degree a certain amount of this was understandable, especially from the theatre sister, who would be carefully monitoring Jo's performance, but she was also aware that she had somehow become the object not only of Lewis Gregson's scrutiny but also that of Marcus Jacobs.

By the end of the morning it seemed to Jo that at no matter what point of an operation she chose to look up one or the other appeared to be watching her.

At last when Jo was finally clearing up after the final patient of the morning's list, Mr Hughes thanked everyone, then left the theatre to change. Instead of following him, Marcus hung back. Lewis was still checking the oxygen cylinders ready for the afternoon session.

'Was there something else, Dr Jacobs?' asked Jo, her gaze meeting Marcus's over their masks.

'Only to say I've got you the form,' he said.

'Form?' For a moment she couldn't think what he meant, thinking it was something to do with the patients and consent forms.

'Yes, your application form,' he went on, 'for the social club. Remember?'

'Oh, that. Oh, yes, of course.' She had forgotten. With all that had happened in the last twenty-four hours it had gone right out of her head.

'You'll be able to come to the Seventies night now,' Marcus went on enthusiastically.

She frowned. 'When did you say it was?'

'Saturday,' he replied.

'Saturday…' She paused, hesitating.

'That isn't a problem, is it?'

'Well, I don't know. It might be.' Her gaze flickered uncertainly to Lewis, who had obviously overheard the whole thing. 'Mr Gregson?' she said hesitantly.

'Saturday?' he said. 'Yes, that should be OK.'

Only too aware of Marcus's incredulous look, Jo said quickly, 'I'll see you later, Dr Jacobs. In the canteen.'

'Oh, right.' Still looking bemused, the houseman took himself off to the changing rooms.

Jo turned back to Lewis. 'You're not on call on Saturday?'

He shook his head. 'No, not this weekend.'

'And you won't be going to the Seventies night yourself?'

'No, it isn't really my cup of tea.'

'I see.' She paused, uncertain quite what to say next.

'Have you brought your bags with you?' he asked, and she thought she detected an uncharacteristic note of anxiety in his voice, almost as if he feared she might have changed her mind.

'Yes, I have.'

'Good. I'll get changed and then I'll meet you in the car park in—what? Half an hour? I've managed to get the afternoon off so that I can get you settled in, then take you to meet the children from their schools and Jamie from his child-minder.'

'You could just give me the house keys if you like,' Jo began, knowing how much time he'd already taken off.

He shook his head. 'No, that wouldn't do,' he said. 'I need to introduce you to the children's teacher and to Sue so that they know it will be you who'll be picking the children up in future.'

'Oh, yes, I see,' said Jo. 'I hadn't thought of that.'

'It's amazing how quickly you get tuned in to this whole child scene,' he commented.

'Didn't you say something about football practice and ballet classes tonight as well?' she asked as together they made their way out of Theatre.

'Oh, Lord, yes,' he said. Drily, he added, 'There you are, you're getting tuned in already.

'I'll meet you later in the car park,' he went on, before he disappeared to his changing room, leaving Jo to make her way to her own.

When a little later Jo reached the staff canteen Marcus was already there. He stood up as she approached his table.

'Oh, good,' he said. 'There you are. What can I get you?'

'I wasn't going to bother…' Glancing down, she saw that he had bought a baguette and coffee for himself.

'Nonsense,' he said. 'You need something after a morning like we've had.'

'I'll get something—' she began, realising that she was indeed hungry after all.

'No, let me. I insist.' He stood up.

'Oh, well, thanks. Just a cup of tea and a cheese sandwich, please.'

He was back in a matter of minutes. 'It's no good,' he said as he placed the tray before her. 'I can't contain my curiosity any longer.'

'Your curiosity?' she said lightly, knowing full well what he meant.

'Yes.' He sat down opposite her. 'I want to know why you felt you had to ask Lewis Gregson's permission to go to the social club on Saturday night.'

'He might have wanted me to work,' Jo replied, unwrapping the Cellophane around her sandwiches.

'Work?' Marcus frowned. 'Are you on call on the day unit?'

'No,' Jo replied.

'Then what...? I don't understand.'

'This is my other job we're talking about,' she said.

'Other job?' He frowned again. 'What's that?'

'I'm to be a sort of nanny to Lewis Gregson's nephews and niece while their mother's away. He overheard me saying I needed more hours and offered me the job.'

'Oh,' said Marcus, 'I see.'

Jo doubted that he did but somehow at that particular moment she didn't want to enlighten him any
further. She really couldn't imagine his reaction
when he heard that not only would she be a living-
in nanny but that Lewis would also be living in the
same house. Instead she decided it was time the subject was changed. 'You said you had an application
form for me,' she said.

'What?' He still looked bemused then his face
cleared. 'Oh, yes,' he said, and from the pocket of
his white coat he drew out a folded sheet of paper
which he passed across the table to her. 'Just fill that
in and let me have it back,' he said. 'Sounds as if
the Seventies night is going to be fun. Everyone's
going, and it seems like they're all prepared to act
the part.'

'I haven't got any Seventies gear,' said Jo.

'None of us have,' Marcus replied with a laugh.
'But there are plenty of charity shops in town.'

'That's a good idea,' said Jo, wondering just when
she was going to get a chance to browse round the
shops.

'While we're on the subject of the Seventies
night,' said Marcus, 'I was wondering, would you
like to come with me?'

She hesitated for only a moment. 'Thank you,
Marcus,' she said. 'I should love to.'

'It's a date, then.' He smiled and then, glancing at
his watch, he stood up. 'I have to go.'

'Thanks for the lunch.'

'Don't mention it. See you tomorrow.'

She watched as he strolled out of the canteen. This would be the first date she'd had since Simon, and while she'd told Pru she was off men at present she knew deep down it was time to move on. They couldn't all be like Simon and, really, it had only been a matter of time before she met someone else. Whether Marcus Jacobs was that someone else she didn't really know, but it might be fun finding out, she told herself with a smile as a few minutes later she, too, stood up and left the canteen.

She and Lewis reached the car park at the same time, and as Jo unlocked the car she realised he was heading for a silver sports car parked in the row behind hers. So that had been his, she thought. The other two vehicles parked on the drive of the house in Mowbery Avenue must have belonged to his sister and her husband.

'I'll follow you,' she called across the tops of the parked cars.

'Yes, OK.' He nodded.

While keeping within the speed limits, Lewis drove faster than she normally did and Jo had trouble keeping up with him as they drove through Queensbury.

Mowbery Avenue looked totally different in the afternoon sunshine, with the cherry blossom in full bloom and the mass of spring flowers in the front gardens, from how it had the previous night in the early dusk. Even the house appeared friendly and inviting now, whereas before it had seemed dark and rather forbidding.

Jo's spirits lifted slightly as she parked her car behind the silver sports model on the drive and climbed out. Maybe it wouldn't be so bad living here after all.

If she was honest she'd had second thoughts since agreeing to take on the job the previous evening. In fact, she'd had an almost sleepless night, worrying about it. She wasn't even sure why she had agreed in the end, especially when she had made up her mind not to do so. She felt it had been something to do with the way Lewis himself had taken on such a mammoth task and the selfless compassion he had shown in the situation. And it hadn't been until she had got home that she had begun to question why she should have felt it necessary to do likewise.

After all, these were Lewis's sister's children. They were family, his family. Nothing whatsoever to do with her. It was understandable that he should feel he would want to help out in such an emergency— why she had felt compelled to do the same thing was beyond her.

But it was too late now, she told herself grimly as she unlocked the boot of her car and dragged out the two bulging holdalls that she had hastily packed the night before. She had said she would help and she wasn't one to break her word.

'Here, let me give you a hand with those.' Lewis came up behind her and took the bags from her, leaving her to bring shoes and the clothes she had left on hangers lying flat in the boot.

She followed him to the front door where briefly he set down one of the bags and inserted the key in the lock. 'Welcome to Chilterns,' he said as the door swung open and he stood back to allow her to precede him into the hall.

This, too, looked different in daytime. Light and airy but at the same time homely and practical with its inevitable selection of baby buggies and toy bikes, and in one corner a solid-looking coat stand loaded with raincoats and anoraks. Underneath was a row of shiny wellington boots of all sizes and colours.

'I'll take these straight up,' said Lewis, heading for the stairs. 'Haven't had a chance to clear up yet today…'

'No, I don't suppose you have,' she replied, following him more slowly up the wide staircase.

'This morning was the usual frantic chaos,' he called over his shoulder. 'Alistair couldn't find his gym shoes. In the end we decided he must have left them at school, then Francesca flatly refused to wear the dress I'd put out for her. When she finally found the one she wanted it was at the bottom of the laundry basket.'

'What did you do?' asked Jo.

'Eventually I persuaded her to wear a pair of leggings and a top,' he said. 'But it was no easy task, I can tell you. Francesca has a mind of her own and when she's made it up about something there's very little shifting her...as you will find out,' he added darkly.

By this time they had reached the landing, where the door to Francesca's bedroom stood wide open.

It had been dark the night before and the little girl had been barely discernible in the glow from the dim nightlight. Now the bed was empty, but bright sunlight spilled across the mermaid motif on the duvet cover and Jo saw that the shelves around the bed were packed with books and games. In one corner was a large doll's house and beside that a toy cot filled with dolls and fluffy animals.

It looked a delightful room but Jo's momentary impression was that these children had everything and were probably spoilt and overindulged.

There was little to alter her opinion as they moved down the passage and passed Alistair's bedroom and she was afforded a glimpse of expensive-looking football gear and a toy computer.

'I'm using Rebecca's and David's room, which is down there.' Lewis nodded to a closed door further down the passage. 'And this is the guest room,' he said, opening a door on the far side of the baby's room.

The room she was to use was blue, lavender blue with white muslin curtains, pine furniture and a white cotton embroidered bedspread.

'Oh, it's lovely!' Jo stood in the doorway, looking around, while Lewis set the bags down on the polished floor under the window.

'Rebecca has exquisite taste,' he said. Turning, he opened the window. 'It needs some fresh air in here,' he added as the breeze caught the soft fabric of the curtains.

Crossing the room, Jo joined him at the window. The room was at the rear of the house and overlooked the garden, which although mostly grass was dotted with a child's swing, slide and a sandpit and was enclosed by a wall of mellow red brick.

'I love walled gardens,' said Jo. 'They feel so medieval.'

'You like history?' He turned his head to look at her.

'Oh, yes, very much, especially anything to do with the Middle Ages—it was such a romantic period.' She paused. 'How about you?'

He nodded. 'Yes, I did history as an optional subject. Somehow it served as a balance to all that science and sport...'

'You like sport?' She half turned.

'Yes, I used to play rugby at university. And rowing—I'm very keen on rowing.'

He turned away from the window. 'I'll leave you,' he said, 'to get yourself sorted out.'

'All right. Thank you.'

'We need to go in about half an hour to collect the children.'

'Yes, of course.' She nodded and continued to stand by the window until, without meeting her gaze again, he left the room.

Turning back to the window, she stared down into the garden.

At the far end beside a little potting shed was a sort of orchard. The blossom on the apple trees was just coming into flower, while against one side of the red brick wall a magnolia tree was gently shedding its petals onto the pathway and on the other an unwieldy clematis tumbled to the ground in a cascade of star-like flowers.

With a little sigh she turned back to the room that was to be hers for the immediate future. Maybe, she thought, with surroundings like this, the whole thing was not going to be nearly so bad as she had at first thought.

After she'd unpacked her clothes and hung them in the pine wardrobe, set out her toiletries on the dressing-table and slipped her nightshirt beneath the lavender-scented pillow, she quickly changed into jeans and a sweater, combed her hair and applied a quick touch of make-up.

Lewis was waiting for her in the hall. He, too, had

changed and was also wearing jeans but with a rugby shirt. In one hand he carried a small pair of football boots and a neatly folded football jersey and in the other a tiny pair of pink ballet shoes. Solemnly he placed them on the hall table.

For some inexplicable reason Jo felt her throat constrict and just for the moment words failed her.

CHAPTER FOUR

FRANCESCA'S nursery school was on the same premises as Alistair's primary school, which made parking the car a little less of a problem than it might have been. They went in David's Range Rover for, as Lewis had explained, there was no way they would all fit into either his sports car or Rebecca's car, not with two young children and a baby, a baby car seat and a buggy.

'You'll be all right when it's just you and the kids,' said Lewis as they climbed out of the vehicle and he locked it. 'There'll be room in your car, or you could take the Range Rover if you like. I'm sure David wouldn't mind.'

'No, thanks,' said Jo hastily. 'I'll stick to mine, I think.'

They met Francesca's teacher first and Lewis introduced Jo as a friend who was helping him to look after the children while their parents were away. 'She will be picking Francesca up most days,' he went on to explain.

Francesca had rushed up to Lewis when they had first entered the room but she hung back now staring suspiciously at Jo.

Jo decided not to rush her. She knew enough about child care to know that if she did so it could be a disaster. Instead she simply smiled at the little girl then took no further notice of her.

It was different in Alistair's classroom because, while the little boy also had a suspicious expression on his face, he recognised Jo. Once again Lewis made the necessary introductions to the boy's class teacher.

'How is Mr Cunningham?' asked the teacher in a lowered voice.

'My sister phoned last night,' Lewis replied, 'and apparently there is no change.'

'It must be terribly worrying for you all,' said the teacher, shaking her head.

'Yes.' Lewis nodded. 'It is, but the best thing we can do for Rebecca is to try to keep things going here as normally as possible while she is away.'

'Yes, of course...' The teacher looked at Jo as if she was wondering just what her role was going to be in bringing this about.

'Jo is a staff nurse at St Theresa's,' said Lewis firmly, as if he had read the unspoken question in the teacher's eyes.

'Really?' The woman seemed to brighten at that, as if Jo's medical qualifications would cover any eventuality.

Outside the building, between them Lewis and Jo helped the two children into the back of the Range

Rover where they secured the seat belts. 'Now,' said Lewis as he climbed into the driver's seat, 'we'll pick Jamie up, then it's home for a drink and a snack before I take Alistair to football practice—'

'And me to ballet!' piped up Francesca from the back seat.

'And you to ballet,' Lewis went on, 'while Jo stays with Jamie.'

'Why has she got a boy's name?' asked Francesca solemnly.

'Why has who got a boy's name?' Lewis was concentrating on the traffic and his answer was preoccupied.

'Her—Jo,' replied Francesca.

'Maybe you'd better ask her yourself,' said Lewis with a sideways glance at Jo.

There was silence from the rear seat then at last, in a very small voice, Francesca said, 'Why have you got a boy's name?'

Jo turned and looked over her shoulder at the two children who were scrutinising her with great interest.

'Actually, it isn't only a boy's name,' she said.

'I know a boy called Joe,' said Alistair.

'I expect his real name is Joseph,' said Jo.

'Is that your real name too?' asked Francesca.

'No.' Jo shook her head. 'My real name is Joanne. But everyone calls me Jo.'

'Why?' said Francesca.

'I don't know really,' Jo admitted. 'Probably because it's easier to say.'

'Mummy sometimes calls me Al,' said Alistair, 'and she calls Francesca Franny, but Daddy never does. Daddy always calls me Alistair.'

'And me Francesca,' the little girl added.

'But we all call Uncle Lewis Lew, even Daddy,' said Alistair.

'Really?' Jo shot a glance at Lewis, and to her amusement she saw that he was looking a bit embarrassed. 'Is that so? Maybe Uncle Lewis would like me to call him Lew as well.'

He didn't answer, instead pulling the Range Rover into the kerb and stopping before a neat, modern, semi-detached house with a bright blue door.

'This is where Sue lives,' said Francesca. 'Sue looks after Jamie,' she explained for Jo's benefit.

It didn't seem much, but to Jo it somehow represented a breakthrough in that at least she and the little girl were now communicating.

Sue Meadows was a pleasant woman in her thirties with two children of her own. Yet again Lewis went through the details of Jo's role in helping the Cunningham family and that in future it would most probably be she who would be picking Jamie up each afternoon.

'He's been very good today,' said Sue. 'But I'm afraid he's slept most of the afternoon.'

'Great,' muttered Lewis as a few minutes later he

secured the baby in his car seat. 'No doubt he's saving his lungs for tonight.'

At last they were heading for Mowbery Avenue. By this time Jamie had woken and was getting fidgety.

'It's nearly time for his feed,' said Francesca with a wisdom beyond her years. Then, with a suddenness that took their breath away, she abruptly changed the subject. 'Alistair says you are Uncle Lew's girlfriend,' she said.

'That isn't true, you know,' said Lewis calmly, without looking at Jo.

'Alistair said you kissed her,' Francesca went on relentlessly. 'Was that true?'

'Yes,' Lewis admitted. 'That was true, but—'

'So why did you kiss her?' Alistair sniggered. 'Kissing is soppy. Ugh! Fancy kissing someone. Especially a girl!'

'I only kissed Jo,' said Lewis patiently, 'because I was happy.'

'Why were you happy?' asked Francesca.

'I was happy because Jo had just said she would help me look after you lot. That's why!'

That seemed for the moment to put paid any further questions and they completed the rest of the journey home in comparative peace.

After a quick cup of tea, and orange juice and biscuits for the children, Lewis bundled the two older ones back into the Range Rover to ferry them to their respective activities, leaving Jo to tend to Jamie who had been gnawing quite happily on a rusk for the last fifteen minutes.

'I'll wait for them,' Lewis had said just before he left. 'There isn't much point in coming back. Alistair's practice is only for an hour and Francesca's class is for forty minutes. You can cope here all right?'

'Oh, yes,' Jo had replied. 'Jamie and I can get to know each other.'

She'd never had dealings with such a young baby before and she was understandably apprehensive as she gazed down at him as he sat in his baby chair. With his solemn, unblinking blue eyes he stared back, then a smile broke out followed by a definite gurgle of pleasure.

'You know, Jamie,' said Jo, bending down and lifting him from the seat, 'I think you and I are going to get along just fine.'

She was to wonder a few times in the next couple of hours whether or not this had been an overly optimistic statement, but somehow she managed to bath the squirming baby, talc and cream him, don a disposable nappy in spite of chubby little legs that worked and kicked as fast as pistons, and dress him in a clean vest and fresh Babygro.

By the time Lewis returned with the children she had fed Jamie his baby cereal and was giving him his last bottle of the day.

Lewis was impressed. 'It takes me much longer than that,' he said, unable to disguise the admiration in his voice, 'and even then most of his bath water ends up on the floor.'

'How was football?' Jo turned to Alistair, a dishevelled Alistair who was bright-eyed with excitement and plastered in mud.

'Brilliant.' He sighed blissfully. 'Mr Carter said if I carry on like I am he'll pick me for the team.'

'Well done,' said Jo. 'Your dad will be pleased with that.'

'Dad's never seen me play,' said Alistair wistfully. 'He's always away.'

'How about your ballet class?' Jo moved Jamie to her other arm and looked over her shoulder at Francesca who was hopping up and down in the centre of the room, supposedly demonstrating what she had learnt.

'We're doing flower fairies,' said the little girl, looking at Jo through the dark tangle of her curls. 'I'm a bluebell.'

'And a very nice bluebell, I'm sure,' said Jo, her gaze briefly meeting Lewis's in a moment which could only be described as one of shared pride.

'I'll go and run their bath,' said Lewis. 'I'm sure their mother baths them separately but I'm afraid I dump them in together. They don't seem to mind...'

'We have water fights,' said Francesca. 'I beat Alistair last time.'

'No, you didn't,' said her brother indignantly.

'Did.'

'Didn't.'

'Right,' said Lewis. 'Upstairs. The pair of you.'

By the time Jo had settled Jamie in his cot and had left him listening happily to his musical elephant and watching his mobile as it swung gently above him, the other two children were in the bath amidst shrieks and squeals as Lewis attempted to wash hair and ears.

'Jo, watch me!' Francesca cried as she caught sight of her standing in the doorway. The little girl proceeded to lift a plastic duck, which had filled with water, high into the air and tip it over her brother's head.

Lewis was kneeling on the floor on a bathmat and he peered over his shoulder at Jo. He was wearing his glasses and she noticed they had become steamed up and one lens was splashed with blue shampoo.

'We like it when Uncle Lewis baths us,' said Alistair. 'He lets us have more bubbles than Mum...'

This statement was borne out by the vast amount of foam that filled the bath and covered not only the children but Lewis himself and the floor, and which floated around the bathroom in large clouds.

'I never seem to get it right,' said Lewis helplessly.

Somehow they all ended up in fits of giggles, then Jo helped to dry the children and was just buttoning

Francesca's pink dressing-gown when Alistair said, 'What's for supper?'

'You don't want supper as well, do you?' gasped Lewis in mock horror.

'Yes, we do,' chorused the children. 'And then lots of stories....'

Somehow, eventually, they got through. The children had their supper, Lewis told Alistair his story and Jo read to Francesca. Finally the house fell quiet.

Lewis and Jo, slumped in kitchen chairs, faced each other across the table.

'I suppose,' she said wearily, 'we need to think about what we are going to eat now.'

'I'd forgotten about us,' he admitted, looking around the kitchen in a distracted sort of way. 'Now, let's think, what is there? I suppose we could defrost something from the freezer...or, on the other hand, we could phone for a pizza.'

'That sounds like a very good idea to me,' said Jo. 'We'll be more organised tomorrow—maybe put something into the slow-cook before we go to work—but for now, well, I'll tidy up and you go and make that phone call.'

'Jo-o!' a call came from upstairs.

'Oh, no,' groaned Lewis. 'I thought that young lady was asleep.'

'Sounds like it's me she wants,' said Jo, opening the kitchen door.

'You are obviously flavour of the month,' said Lewis.

Walking into the hall, Jo looked up the stairs. 'What do you want, Francesca?' she said, not too loudly for fear of disturbing the other two.

'You didn't kiss me goodnight,' came a small voice from above.

'Yes, Francesca, I did,' said Jo patiently.

'Want another kiss.'

'All right. Just one more and then you must promise to go to sleep.' Silence followed. 'Do you promise, Francesca?'

'Yes.'

'Very well. I'll come up.'

'I'll make that phone call,' said Lewis from close behind her. 'Don't be long.'

'OK.' Jo smiled at him over the bannisters.

'I miss Mummy,' said Francesca a moment later when Jo was sitting on the side of her bed.

'Yes, darling,' said Jo, bending down to kiss her, 'I expect you do. But let's hope she'll be home soon. And your daddy,' she added, hoping that the little girl wouldn't ask too many questions about her father's condition. 'But now I want you to go to sleep like a good girl.'

'All right,' said Francesca, wriggling her small body down under the duvet.

'Goodnight, then,' said Jo.

'Night, Jo.' There was a silence, then the small voice said tentatively, 'Jo?'

'Yes, Francesca?'

'I've had an idea.'

'And what's your idea?'

'We could pretend...you could be our mummy and Uncle Lew could be our daddy, couldn't you?'

'Well, yes, I suppose we could,' said Jo. 'Only until your real mummy and daddy come home,' she added. But by then the little girl's eyelids had closed and Jo suspected she hadn't even heard her.

'Is she all right?' asked Lewis when Jo got back to the kitchen.

'Yes, she's fine,' Jo replied. 'Just wanted a bit of reassurance, I think.' She paused, watching Lewis as he uncorked a bottle of red wine. 'And you can't blame her for that, poor little mite. It must be very confusing for her at the moment—for them all really but, well, probably more for Francesca than any of them. Jamie is too young to understand. Provided his basic needs are satisfied and he has plenty of cuddles, he's all right. And Alistair, well, being a bit older, I dare say he understands a little more than Francesca.'

'They all seem to have taken to you. I say.' Lewis paused and looked up. 'I hope you like red wine?'

'Love it.'

'Good. I thought it would go with the pizza when it arrives and, besides, I think we've earned it.' He handed her a glass. Just for a fraction of a second his fingers brushed hers. No doubt it was accidental but Jo found herself looking up, her gaze meeting his.

'Like I was saying,' he carried on quickly, too quickly really, as if the touching had somehow embarrassed him, 'they really seem to have taken to you.'

'They were wary at first,' she replied. 'Especially Francesca.'

'That was understandable, but you were great with them—so natural—and you didn't rush them, just let them respond to you in their own time.'

'I have had a few dealings with children before, you know.'

'Yes, well.' He looked awkward. 'I just wanted to say thank you, Jo. Thank you for agreeing to come here and help me.'

'That's OK.' She shrugged.

'I know you didn't really want to…' he said.

'Well, I…'

'There's no need to pretend,' he said quietly, leaning back against one of the worktops, his long legs thrust out before him as he carefully examined the contents of his wine glass. 'I know you nearly backed out last night. And, to be honest,' he carried on when she remained silent, 'I wouldn't have blamed you. It must have sounded a pretty daunting prospect. But I want you to know…I really am grateful to you. I don't quite know what I would have done if you'd said no.'

'You'd have found someone,' she mumbled. Her voice sounded slightly husky and she cleared her throat, trying to get it back to normal.

'Maybe.' He shrugged and took a mouthful of his wine. 'But I doubt it would have been the same—'

Mercifully the doorbell rang at that moment, heralding the arrival of their supper, and to Jo's relief the conversation was abandoned.

What was left of the evening passed uneventfully and at last, dog-tired, Jo fell into bed between the lavender-scented sheets in the room overlooking the garden, and almost immediately fell into a deep sleep.

She awoke to bright sunlight and the sounds of children's high-pitched voices and lay for a moment, wondering where on earth she was. As memory flooded back she gave a little groan and stretched. Then she sat up and swung her feet to the floor. A quick glance at her bedside clock revealed that it was six-thirty.

Luckily her room had its own shower unit so she wasn't forced to queue for the bathroom. Half an hour later, showered and dressed but with her hair still wet, she left her bedroom. She could hear the children downstairs but a quick glance into the nursery revealed that Jamie was still asleep. Lying on his back, little hands on either side of his head and fin-

gers loosely curled, he looked peaceful and slightly
flushed with sleep. Leaving the room and pulling the
door to behind her, Jo ran lightly down the stairs and
into the kitchen.

Alistair and Francesca were seated at the table
each with a bowl of cereal in front of them. They
both looked up eagerly as she entered the room.

'I've got hoops this morning,' announced
Francesca.

'Your hair's wet,' said Alistair. 'You can borrow
Mummy's hair-dryer if you like. Can't she, Uncle
Lew?'

'Yes, of course she can.' Lewis had been standing
at the sink with his back to the door but he turned
then. 'Good morning, Jo.'

'Morning…' She trailed off, slightly taken aback
at how shattered he looked. 'It's OK, I do have my
own drier.' She paused. 'I see Jamie is still asleep.'

'He needs to be,' muttered Lewis darkly.

'What do you mean?' Jo looked quickly from
Lewis to the children, who both giggled, then back
to Lewis again. 'Was he awake in the night?'

'You could say that,' Lewis replied, running his
hand over his short hair. 'In fact, I guess you could
go so far as to say he was awake more than he was
asleep.'

'Oh, Lewis.' Jo stared at him, appalled. 'I had no
idea. I never heard a thing.'

'Don't worry about it. I didn't used to hear him at

first. Alistair used to come and wake me up to tell me he was crying. Didn't you, old chap?'

Alistair looked up, shovelling the last of the hoops into his mouth, and nodded.

'But I was only in the next room, for goodness' sake,' said Jo. 'I really should have heard him.'

'Like I say, don't worry about it. Just enjoy it while you can. You'll get used to it soon enough, believe me. I did. Besides, I can't expect you to see to him during the night as well as during the day.'

'Why not?' demanded Jo as she sat down at the table and helped herself to cereal.

'That wasn't really part of the deal. You have a job to go to. You need your sleep.'

'You have a job to go to as well,' she retorted.

'I knew that when I took it on, but...' He stopped, lifting his head to listen, 'Sounds like he's just woken up.'

'I'll get him.' Jo jumped to her feet. As she did so her hand caught the cereal packet, knocking it over and spilling its contents across the kitchen table.

'No,' said Lewis patiently as the children shrieked with mirth. 'I'll get him. You finish your breakfast.'

Somehow they got themselves sorted out—the children finished breakfast and got dressed for school, Jamie was fed and changed, the washing-machine and the dishwasher were loaded and the meat which had been taken from the freezer the previous night was set to cook in the slow-cooker.

And at last they piled into the cars—Jo in her car with the children and Lewis following behind in his sports car. They dropped all three children off at Sue's house as had previously been arranged.

'Who will pick me up after school?' asked Alistair anxiously.

'I will,' said Jo firmly. 'And you, Francesca,' she added, in case the little girl was also worried. But Francesca seemed not to have a care in the world as she made a beeline for the Wendy house in the corner of Sue's living room.

Moments later both cars were heading for St Theresa's.

'All ready for work?' asked Lewis as a little later in the staff car park he locked his car and Jo climbed out of hers.

'I feel like I've already done a day's work,' she replied with a sigh.

'How did it go?' asked Pru curiously.

The two of them were setting up the trolleys, ready for the morning's list.

'I'll let you know when my feet have touched the ground,' said Jo with a rueful grin.

'That bad, eh?' said Pru sympathetically.

'No.' Jo paused, reflecting. 'Not actually that bad. In fact, it's rather good. Different. You could say stimulating in a funny sort of way.'

'By stimulating do you mean exhausting?' Pru raised a cynical eyebrow.

'No...well, maybe you'd better ask me that again in a week or so's time. I could well be on my knees by then,' Jo gave a short laugh then, growing serious again, she went on, 'I tell you what, though, Pru, I really do take my hat off to working mothers—and fathers, come to that. I just don't know how they cope on a long-term basis. At least I know this is only temporary.'

'You don't know for how long, I suppose?' asked Pru as she took packs of supplies from the cupboard.

'No, not really.' Jo shook her head. 'The children's father is apparently very seriously ill. So ill that he can't be moved. Obviously his wife doesn't want to leave him in that condition.'

'You say she's Lewis Gregson's sister?' said Pru thoughtfully, and when Jo nodded in reply she added, 'They really must be close for him to have taken on what he has.'

'I don't think there was anyone else,' said Jo. 'But, yes, you're right. I think they are very close anyway.'

'What's the house like?'

'It's lovely. One of those old, red-brick houses over on Mowbery Avenue, complete with an orchard and a walled garden.'

'Heavens!' said Pru. 'They're not short of a bob or two, then. What are the kids like? Precocious little brats?'

'Actually, no,' said Jo. 'Just the opposite, in fact. They're lovely.'

'Again, maybe that's something I should ask you after a week or so. You may have changed your opinion of them by then.'

Jo smiled but somehow she had the feeling that wouldn't be the case.

'And what about our Mr Anaesthetist?' asked Pru lightly.

'What about him?' said Jo.

'Well, what's he like at home? Is he solemn, quiet, morose even as he appears in Theatre?'

'He isn't morose,' Jo protested. 'Quiet maybe, but certainly not morose.'

'Defending him, are we?' Pru teased, a touch of mischief in her voice now.

'No, not really.' Jo felt her cheeks beginning to grow warm. 'It's just that I guess I've seen another side of him, that's all.'

'You mean changing nappies and reading stories as opposed to putting folk to sleep?'

'Something like that, yes.' Jo nodded, wishing Pru would let the subject drop. Quite suddenly she found she didn't want to discuss Lewis or the domestic arrangements at Mowbery Avenue. Somehow it seemed that to do so would appear disloyal.

'What do we have this morning?' she asked in a determined attempt to change the subject.

'Was I right, though?' Pru, however, seemed to have other ideas.

'About what?' asked Jo with a frown.

'About him being hunky under those theatre greens?'

'I wouldn't know,' she protested.

'Surely he doesn't wear them at home?' Pru gave a peal of laughter. 'Not at the meal table or when he comes out of the bathroom?'

'Of course not,' snapped Jo.

'Well, then. So what does he wear?'

'What do you think he wears?' She was getting exasperated now. 'He wears jeans and rugby shirts or T-shirts, the same as everyone else.'

'Mmm,' murmured Pru appreciatively. 'So, what does he look like in denims and a rugby shirt?'

'I don't know. Sort of...'

'Hunky?' said Pru, raising her eyebrows.

'Well...yes, I suppose so,' said Jo. Then, seeing the funny side of it, she laughed and the pair of them dissolved into a fit of giggles.

'Is there a problem in here?' a voice suddenly interrupted them. They swung round to find Lewis Gregson standing in the doorway, already in his theatre greens.

'Oh, Lord,' said Pru helplessly, trying desperately to control herself. 'No, of course not, Mr Gregson. We were just about to get scrubbed up, weren't we, Jo?'

'Yes.' Jo nodded, equally helpless now but desperately hoping that Lewis was not in any way aware that he had been the reason for their mirth. Somehow she found she couldn't bear it if he was to think that.

CHAPTER FIVE

THE first operation of the morning was an arthroscopy on a young man with a torn semilunar knee cartilage.

'This patient originally presented with pain, joint locking and swelling,' explained Mr Hughes to the team, as he performed two small incisions on either side of the knee.

'A footballer, I presume?' said Marcus as he leaned forward for a better view.

Mr Hughes nodded then, taking the telescopic instrument to which Jo had attached water and suction tubes, he began to examine the site.

'We'll do a washout here, please, Nurse, then I can remove the loose pieces of cartilage. All well at your end, Lewis?'

'Yes, fine, Edward,' Lewis replied.

'Fancy a spot of sailing this weekend, old chap?' Mr Hughes didn't even look up as he spoke, continuing to peer into the wound as with a long-handled pair of scissors he carefully began to remove tiny, sharp pieces of cartilage. 'My brother's taking his company yacht down to the Solent. Thought you might like to join the crew.'

'Would have loved to,' said Lewis. 'Unfortunately I can't, I'm afraid. Not this weekend.'

'On call, old man?' said Mr Hughes, his tone one of understanding sympathy.

'No.'

'Oh?' The surgeon looked up then, as if amazed that there could be anything else that could prevent a weekend's sailing. 'What, then?'

'Rather complicated domestic arrangements,' Lewis replied.

'What, a young single chap like you?' protested the surgeon as the rest of the team also began to show interest. 'You don't know the meaning of domestic arrangements.'

'I'm afraid that isn't strictly true at the present time,' said Lewis. 'My sister has been called away and I'm having to help out with her children.'

He still looked desperately tired and Jo found herself wondering how he was managing to concentrate after having had so little sleep.

'Good Lord!' Mr Hughes sounded appalled. 'Bad enough when it's one's own, but someone else's—well!'

'It's not for ever,' said Lewis as he adjusted the patient's oxygen mask.

'Could we have a swab here, please, Nurse?'

As Jo glanced up she saw a frown above Marcus's mask and she could tell he was trying to work out just what Lewis's involvement was with the children that she was supposed to be looking after.

'That's looking much healthier,' said the surgeon at last as he straightened up. 'Now, we need to pump some local anaesthetic in here, then it's sutures and dressings please.'

The morning's list ground on with another arthroscopy, a hernia and two ingrowing toenails. When at last it was over Jo heard Mr Hughes ask Lewis if he cared to join him for lunch.

'Yes, thank you, Edward. I'll join you in a moment. I just need a word with Staff Nurse first.'

Jo was clearing up and looked up quickly as Lewis leaned across the operating table.

'What is it?' she said, thinking he was about to ask something about one of the patients.

'I've been thinking,' he said seriously. 'We've run out of disposable nappies and I don't think I'll have time to get to the shops.'

She smiled. 'Don't worry. I'll pick some up from the chemist on the way home before I get the children.' She paused. 'Is there anything else we need?'

'I don't think so... Oh, wait a minute, the orange juice was getting a bit low this morning.'

'I'll get that as well.'

'Thanks, Jo.' He smiled and just for a moment he looked relaxed and happier than Jo had yet seen him.

'I thought,' said Marcus as Lewis turned and

walked from the theatre, 'that you said you were looking after those children.'

'I am,' said Jo.

'So why did he say he was?'

'We are sort of doing it between us,' she said quickly. 'Taking it in turns if you like.' She still didn't want to explain that she was living in the same house as Lewis Gregson, fearing that, as Pru had said, it might be misconstrued by people. That was the last thing she wanted, and certainly not by Marcus.

'Oh,' he said. 'I see.' Then, as if he was bored by the whole thing, he said, 'Did you fill in your application form?'

'Oh, Marcus, no.' She stared at him. 'I'm sorry. I didn't have a chance last night.' How could she tell him she had completely forgotten, that with everything else that had been going on it had gone right out of her head?

'Well, you'd better hurry up if you want to go to the Seventies night.' He sounded slightly miffed. 'That is, I take it you still want to go?'

'Oh yes, Marcus. I do. Of course I do. It's just that... Look, I tell you what, I'll fill it in now before I go off duty.'

'Yes, well. It has to be vetted.' He still sounded a bit put out.

'I am sorry,' Jo said again. 'I promise I'll do it and let you have it before I go. I'm looking forward to the Seventies night,' she added in a further attempt to make up for not having completed the form before. 'I must talk to Pru about what I am going to wear.'

After changing she hastily fished the form out of her shoulder-bag, where she had put it the day before. She unfolded it, smoothed out the creases and filled it in. Realising she needed someone to sponsor her, she hurried out of the changing room and made her way to the nurses' station where she found Pru talking to Julian Browne.

'All finished for today?' said Julian as she approached.

'Yes,' she replied, then, with a quick smile at Pru, she added, 'Well, here at least. Pru, would you sign my application form for the social club, please?'

'Course I will.' Pru took the pen that Julian passed to her, and while she was signing the form Julian said. 'Are you coming to the Seventies night?'

'Hopefully, yes,' Jo replied, 'if my application is approved.'

'Oh, it will be,' said Julian. 'That's just a formality.'

'You'll come with me, won't you, Jo?' Pru said as she handed the form back.

'Well, actually…' Jo hesitated. 'Someone else has already asked me.'

'Who, Lewis Gregson?' said Pru quickly.

'No. No, not Lewis.'

'Who, then?' Pru's eyes narrowed slightly.

'Marcus, actually.'

Pru stared at her, then in mild exasperation she said. 'Honestly, Jo Henry, what is it with you? You've only been in the place five minutes and you've got them all eating out of your hand...'

'Oh, hardly,' Jo protested, feeling her cheeks redden under Julian's amused glance.

'Well, there's Lewis Gregson who, to my knowledge, has never as much as opened his mouth to any other woman on this unit, and now Marcus—'

'Who by your own admission chats up everyone,' Jo interrupted. 'Come on, Pru, be fair. And as for Lewis, you can hardly count that. You know what that's all about.'

With that, to Jo's relief, Pru laughed, and what for a moment had seemed like animosity between them was over.

'I hope,' said Julian, 'that you are going to enter into the spirit of this and wear the appropriate clothing.'

'Ah, now, that's what I was going to ask you about,' said Jo. 'Any suggestions where I might get any Seventies gear?'

'There's a charity shop in the precinct,' said Pru. 'The one opposite Woolworths. If you go through to the back room they have a wonderful selection of flares, kaftans and frilly shirts. Why don't you pop in there on your way home?'

'Yes.' Jo nodded. 'Maybe I will.' If I have the

time, she thought, between buying disposable nappies and orange juice and picking up one baby and two small children.

'You're the fifth one today after Seventies gear,' said the woman in the charity shop with a laugh. 'Is this for the do at St Theresa's?'

'Yes, it is,' Jo replied. 'I don't suppose you've got much left now if everyone else has been in.'

'What size are you?' The woman had narrowed her eyes and was eyeing Jo up and down.

'A size ten usually,' said Jo.

'That's what I thought,' said the woman. 'There is one dress through there.' She indicated the curtain that separated the main shop from the room at the back that Pru had told Jo about. 'Everyone wanted it, but it was too small. I reckon it would fit you, though. Come and see.'

The dress was calf-length chiffon in varying shades of green with a low neckline, full cape sleeves and a hemline of softly floating handkerchief points.

'I remember my mother wearing a dress like that to a ladies night,' said Jo.

'Do you want to try it on?'

'I don't have the time,' Jo replied with a frantic glance at her watch. 'But it looks as if it will fit. I think I'll take it and chance it.'

'You can bring it back if it doesn't fit,' said the

woman. 'But if it does you'll look stunning with your blonde hair.'

Half an hour later Jo drew up outside Sue Meadows's house.

Jamie was lying on a rug on the floor, kicking and gurgling and trying to ram a plastic dog into his mouth. 'How has he been today?' asked Jo as Sue bent down to pick him up.

'No trouble at all,' said Sue. 'Like a little angel.'

'I doubt his uncle would agree with you after last night,' said Jo with a laugh.

'Oh, dear,' said Sue. 'Bad night?'

'You could say that.' Jo nodded. 'I'm ashamed to say I didn't hear a thing. I slept through it all.'

'So...you are actually staying at Mowbery Avenue with Mr Gregson?' said Sue. 'I hadn't realised that.'

'Yes,' said Jo. 'That's what Mr Gregson needed. Someone who could be there with the children if he's called out to the hospital in the night.'

'I thought he was on the day unit,' said Sue as she began to gather up Jamie's belongings.

'Well, yes, he is,' said Jo. 'And they, of course, don't operate through the night, but most anaesthetists are on a duty rota which means they are on call for the general theatre as well and, of course, that includes emergencies.'

'Oh, I see,' said Sue. 'Yes, that must be a problem for him. I think it was brilliant the way he took over when Mrs Cunningham had to go—I can't see many men in his situation doing the same thing. Let's face it, it isn't as if he has children of his own, is it?'

'That's true,' Jo agreed. 'But I have to say, the children do seem to adore him.'

'Oh, I'm sure they do,' said Sue quickly. 'Don't get me wrong, and I'm sure he thinks the world of them. All I'm saying is that it can't have been easy for him. But now…well, now he has you there, and I'm sure that will make a world of difference.'

'Well, it might do,' said Jo, 'that is, if I can manage to actually wake up when Jamie cries in the night.'

'I would say that's probably only a matter of time,' said Sue with a laugh as she handed the baby over.

By the time Jo had secured Jamie in his car seat and stowed his bag and buggy in the boot, she was beginning to think that Pru might have been right when she had said that others might misconstrue the facts over her and Lewis Gregson living in the same house.

This was borne out even further when she reached the nursery school. It had already been explained that she would have to go right into the building to fetch Francesca as the children were not permitted to leave the premises unless accompanied by an authorised person. This, to Jo, was fully acceptable but at the same time it necessitated her taking Jamie from his car seat and carrying him into the building with her as she could hardly leave him alone in the car even if it was only for a short length of time.

Francesca gave a squeal of delight when she caught sight of Jo.

'There she is,' she cried. 'That's her. That's Jo!'

'She's been telling us all day that it would be you coming to fetch her today,' said the teacher with a laugh.

'Has she?' said Jo. Suddenly she found she was inordinately pleased by the fact. 'Hello, Francesca.' She smiled down at the little girl who was hopping up and down in excitement and making Jamie laugh. 'Have you had a nice day?'

'Yes. I did a picture for you.' Proudly the little girl held up the painting for Jo to see.

'That's lovely,' said Jo as she gazed at the two splodges, one black and the other white. 'Are they penguins or seagulls?'

'Don't be silly!' said Francesca scornfully. 'That one is you...' she pointed to the white splodge '...and that one is Uncle Lew.'

'Oh,' said Jo, slightly taken aback. 'I see. Well, that's very nice, I'm sure.'

'I understand congratulations are in order,' said the teacher as she took the painting and rolled it up.

'Congratulations?' asked Jo, mystified.

'Yes, Francesca told us about you and her uncle.'

'Her uncle...?'

'About you getting married. That's what her painting is. Oh, dear.' She paused as she caught sight of Jo's expression. 'Do we have yet another child's flight of fancy on our hands?'

'Yes.' Jo nodded. 'I'm afraid you do.'

'So you and Mr Gregson aren't...?'

'No, absolutely not. Mr Gregson is simply my employer at the moment. All I'm doing is helping him out while the children's mother is away.'

'Isn't it strange how children get hold of these ideas,' said the teacher. 'One wonders where they come from.'

'Well, Francesca did say she wanted to pretend that Lew—Mr Gregson and myself were her parents,' said Jo, looking down at Francesca who was following the conversation intently.

'I wonder why?' mused the teacher.

'Alistair said Jo is Uncle Lew's girlfriend,' Francesca piped up suddenly. 'That's why I thought it would be nice if they got married.'

'Goodness me,' said Jo. 'I can't think what gave him that idea.'

'Because Uncle Lew kissed you,' said Francesca solemnly.

'Is that so?' said the teacher, who by this time was quite obviously having to struggle to keep a straight face.

'I think,' said Jo, 'it's time to go and find Alistair.'

Leaving the teacher laughing and shaking her

head, they made their way out of the building and across a large grassy area to the primary school.

By this time Jamie was getting heavy and Jo's arms were beginning to ache. She hadn't realised she would have to carry him for such a length of time.

'Does Mummy carry Jamie when you go to meet Alistair?' she asked Francesca as the little girl squatted on the grass and began to pick daisies.

'No.' Francesca shook her head. 'She puts him in his buggy.'

'Now, why didn't I think of that,' said Jo ruefully.

At that moment, together with about a dozen other small children, Alistair rushed out of his classroom. When he caught sight of the little group on the grass he stopped abruptly then seemed to hang back.

''Lo, Alistair,' called Francesca.

'Had a good day?' asked Jo.

'Sort of,' muttered Alistair. He looked miserable now, desperate even, and Jo suddenly felt sorry for him. He also must be missing his mother. Maybe he had forgotten for the moment that she was away. Maybe he had expected her to be waiting for him and, seeing Jo there, it had been a terrible disappointment. Carefully she settled Jamie more comfortably on her hip, and as they began to walk across the grass again she put her hand down and took hold of his. Immediately he yanked it away.

'Don't do that,' he said through clenched teeth.

'Sorry,' said Jo. 'Why not?'

'They might see.' Furtively Alistair glanced over his shoulder at his classmates and Jo saw that he had flushed to the very tips of his ears. 'Why did you have to come right up to the classroom?' he muttered desperately.

'I'm sorry,' said Jo again. 'I thought that's what your mum did.'

'No,' said Alistair angrily. 'She waits over there.' He nodded across the grass to a pathway on the far side, close to the gates, where Jo could now see a number of the other mothers were waiting.

'I didn't know,' said Jo.

'She knew,' said Alistair, prodding his sister.

'Why didn't you say, Francesca?' prompted Jo.

'I wanted to pick the daisies,' said Francesca.

'I think I've got a lot to learn about children,' said Jo ruefully.

It was later that night, the children had all been bathed and fed and were in bed. Jo and Lewis were sitting at the kitchen table, eating the remains of the casserole, and Jo had just related the story of picking the children up from school.

'Haven't we all?' he said drily.

'Well, at least I know now for the future,' said Jo.

'It's to do with understanding their own separate little worlds,' said Lewis, 'and recognising them each as individuals. I learnt quite early on that you can't just lump them all together.'

He paused then glanced up at the wall next to the noticeboard, where Francesca had demanded that Jo hang her painting. 'Do you know what that is?' he said with a wry smile.

'Oh, yes.' Jo nodded. 'I actually had it explained to me by her teacher who had just congratulated me.'

'I wonder why she painted that?' mused Lewis, leaning back in his chair as he finished his meal.

'I think it might have been something to do with the fact that last night when I put her to bed she said she wanted to pretend that I was her mum and you were her dad—maybe she simply went one stage further and thought if that was the case we should be married.'

Lewis chuckled. 'They could get you hung, couldn't they, young children?'

'You can say that again,' Jo smiled. 'She had even told her teacher that Alistair had said I must be your girlfriend because you had kissed me.'

'Oh, not that again.' Lewis stared at her then they were both forced to laugh. 'So it's only a matter of time before the gossip starts. You know the sort of thing—not only are we living under the same roof...'

'That sort of thing doesn't bother me,' said Jo as she began to clear the plates. When Lewis didn't answer she threw him a glance. 'It doesn't bother you, does it?' she asked curiously. She found it hard to believe that he would be bothered by something like that, but one could never be sure.

'No, not really.' He paused. 'But I have to say I don't particularly like situations being misconstrued.' He stopped abruptly as the phone suddenly rang behind him. Leaning back, he lifted the receiver to answer the call. Jo continued to clear the table, stacking the plates in the dishwasher. When she had nearly finished Lewis replaced the receiver then stood up.

'That was the hospital,' he said. 'I'm sorry but I have to go in. They've got an emergency on.'

'That's OK. You go—'

'That means leaving you with everything—'

'That's the whole point of my being here.'

'Well, yes, but…'

'Go on,' she said. 'I'll see you later.'

'It could be much later. On the other hand, it might not be too long—there's really no telling.'

After Lewis had gone Jo completed all the jobs that still needed doing, including a huge pile of ironing. When she had finished she decided she might as well get ready for bed.

After taking a bath, she looked in on the children. Mercifully they were all sound asleep. Alistair had burrowed right down under his duvet, while Francesca had kicked her cover onto the floor. Only Jamie was in the same position as Jo had left him when she had put him to bed. After straightening the two older children out and tidying their covers, she was about to get into bed when she saw the bag from the charity shop, which she had put on her bedroom floor on returning home and promptly forgotten about.

Opening the bag, she took out the green chiffon dress and shook it out, deciding that in spite of her tiredness she really should try it on. If it didn't fit she would have to return it the following day and try to find something else.

Almost half-heartedly, she pulled the dress over her head and let it fall around her, smoothing it down over her breasts and hips. It fitted her perfectly, almost as if it had been made for her.

There was a full-length mirror on the inside of the wardrobe door and, opening the door, Jo stood back to look at herself. There had been something about the feel of the dress that she had liked as she had put it on and now, as she stared at her reflection, she found that in spite of the fact that the fashion was dated the style really did suit her. She decided there and then that it would be more than suitable for the Seventies night.

She was about to unzip it again when she heard the sound of a whimper from Jamie's room. She listened, then moved to the door, opened it and listened again. If Jamie wanted a drink or to have his nappy changed, better she did it now then wait until she had just got to sleep and have him wake her.

For the moment all was still and quiet and Jo was just thinking she must have imagined that she had heard him when she heard the sound again. This time she moved down the passage to his room and gently pushed open the door.

The baby was still asleep, however, and even as Jo watched from the doorway he called out again, waving his arms in the air and moving his head from side to side. She continued to watch him for a while then he grew still again and the only sound to be heard was the gentle sound of his breathing. As Jo at last backed from the room she heard another noise, this time from downstairs—the unmistakable sound of a key in the lock.

Swiftly she moved onto the landing and looked down the stairs. Lewis was standing in the hall, quietly closing the front door. As he turned from the door Jo was struck by how utterly weary he looked, and her heart went out to him as she remembered how little sleep he'd had the night before, followed by a full day in Theatre, then helping her with the children and now this case of emergency surgery.

He turned and something seemed to compel him to look up. Jo smiled in greeting, fully expecting him to do the same. Instead, he simply stood there as if transfixed and stared at her.

'Lewis…?' Puzzled, she moved forward out of the shadow into the light from the lamp on the hall table. As he continued to stare at her she very slowly began to descend the stairs. 'Is there anything wrong?' she said.

'What?' He seemed to shake himself slightly, as

if coming out of a trance. 'No,' he said. 'No, there's nothing wrong...'

'Why are you looking at me like that?'

'I'm sorry, Jo,' he said at last. 'It's just... you...that dress... You look wonderful.'

CHAPTER SIX

SOMETHING stirred deep inside Jo as she stood there on the stairs and stared at Lewis. She wasn't sure what it was—she only knew it was a direct response to the expression in his eyes. Then the moment was over and she hurried down to the hall to join him.

'Well, thank you,' she said, trying hard to keep her voice light but at the same time finding it difficult even to speak. 'I bought it today—in a charity shop, would you believe? It's vintage Seventies in case you were wondering, all ready for the night at the social club on Saturday.' She paused, suddenly afraid she was beginning to waffle. 'How did the emergency go?' she added, deciding on an impulse that a change of subject was needed.

'OK.' He shrugged. 'It was a perforated duodenal ulcer. Er...have the kids been all right?'

'Yes, fine. Would you like a hot drink?'

'I'll get it...'

'No, I'll do it. You look all in.'

'I am pretty shattered,' he admitted as he followed her into the kitchen.

'You must be,' she said as she poured milk into a saucepan. 'You've had quite a time of it in the last twenty-four hours.' She paused as she took two mugs out of the cupboard and opened a tin of drinking chocolate. 'If Jamie wakes tonight, I'll see to him.'

When Lewis raised an eyebrow she added, 'I'll leave my bedroom door open. I should hear him, then. You shut yours so there's a good chance you won't.'

'You know, I think I might just take you up on that offer,' he said, watching her as she poured the warm milk into the mugs.

'I think you have to,' she said. 'You're not super-human and you do have a job to do—a very impor-tant job at that.'

'Your job's not exactly a doddle,' he said, taking the mug from her.

'No, well, if we take these night shifts in turns it should make life easier for us both.'

'OK. You win.' He smiled up at her, and not for the first time she was struck by the warmth of his smile and of something else, something again in the expression in his eyes, but before she could even begin to explore what that might be he spoke again. 'That dress really is lovely, you know.'

'I was lucky to get it,' she said, turning away from him in sudden confusion and picking up her own mug. 'They didn't have a lot of Seventies gear left— it seems everyone else had been in before me.'

'Are you looking forward to it?' he asked sud-denly.

'The Seventies night? Yes, I suppose so. I haven't really had much time to think about it.'

'Are you going with Marcus Jacobs?' He spoke lightly but Jo detected an edge to his voice that she'd never heard before.

'Er…yes. Why?'

'Oh, no reason. I just wondered, that's all.' He took a sip of his drink. 'It's just that…'

'Yes?' she said. 'What?'

'Oh, nothing. Nothing, really.'

'No, go on. What were you going to say?'

'I wasn't going to say anything,' he protested.

'Yes, you were. You started saying "It's just that…" then you stopped. What were you going to say? It's just that what?'

'He has a bit of a reputation, that's all.'

'Marcus Jacobs?'

'Yes.'

'I can look after myself, you know,' she said firmly.

'I'm sure you can. I'd just hate you to get hurt.'

'Oh, you needn't worry about that,' said Jo almost flippantly. 'There's no way I'm going to let that happen again—' She broke off abruptly. She hadn't meant to say that. She threw Lewis a sharp glance, hoping he hadn't heard, but there was no chance of that.

'You mean it already has?' he said quietly.

She nodded. 'Yes.'

'Recently?'

'It was the reason I came to Queensbury.'

'Ah, I see. Fresh start and all that?'

'Something like that. Yes.' She swallowed. It still hurt to think about it. Even more to talk about it.

'So it was serious, then?'

'I thought it was. Simon—that was his name—obviously had other ideas, as I found out to my cost.'

'Want to talk about it?'

'No. I don't think so. I don't know.' She shrugged.

'It helps, you know,' he said quietly.

She looked up quickly. Lewis was still watching her carefully. Unable to meet his gaze, she looked away again. 'You sound as if you know,' she said.

'Maybe I do.'

'So do *you* want to talk about it?' She spoke spontaneously, but even as she said the words she found herself wondering about him, curious about who it was who had hurt him.

'Mine was a long time ago,' he said. 'I've had time to heal. Yours is obviously recent and therefore still raw. Healing is gradual—it takes time.'

He was silent then, and she knew he was waiting for her to speak.

'He was a doctor,' she said at last. 'A houseman at the last hospital I was in. In Berkshire. I fell head over heels in love with him and I thought he felt the same way about me. We went out together for about six months. Then one weekend I went home to see my parents. I came back to Berkshire a day early. I went to his flat, thinking I would surprise him, thinking he would be pleased to see me. He was in bed with one of the telephonists from the hospital.'

'I'm sorry…' said Lewis.

'D'you know the worst part?' said Jo as she felt the tears fill her eyes. 'It was when he thought we could carry on afterwards where we had left off. As if it didn't matter. As if none of it mattered. He really didn't understand when he told me that she didn't mean anything to him and I told him that if that was the case then I didn't mean anything to him either.'

'It hurts, doesn't it?' There was deep sympathy in his eyes now.

'Yes.' She nodded, wiping the tears from her cheek with the back of her hand. 'Is that what happened to you?' She looked at him curiously and saw a tiny nerve throbbing near the edge of his jaw.

'Very similar,' he admitted at last, 'the difference being we were actually engaged. And the guy I found out she was two-timing me with was my best friend.'

'Oh, God, that's even worse,' said Jo with a gulp.

'Well, like I say, it was all a very long time ago.' He gave a shrug. 'And I can assure you I've been very careful not to let the same thing happen again.'

'And so shall I be very careful,' said Jo. 'I don't want to go through anything like that again.'

Draining his mug, he stood up. 'I guess I'll turn in,' he said with a yawn. 'Thanks for the drink.'

'Goodnight, Lewis.'

'Goodnight, Jo.'

In spite of being tired, Jo found it difficult to sleep when she eventually got to bed.

To start with she found herself lying there listening for Jamie, but it wasn't only that. She also found herself turning over and over in her mind what Lewis Gregson had revealed to her about his private life—his engagement and the reason for its break-up. It somehow added a dimension to this man's life of which, Jo now realised, she'd known absolutely nothing.

As the hands on her bedside clock moved to midnight Jo wondered what sort of woman his fiancée had been, wondered what sort of woman attracted him. He had said that she, Jo, looked wonderful in the green dress. Maybe that was an indication that he liked his women blonde and of a slight build. On the other hand, maybe it had simply been the dress which had caught his fancy.

He had tried to warn her about Marcus, had said he didn't want her to get hurt. No doubt he knew Marcus of old. She smiled to herself in the darkness. Simon had hurt her, had hurt her badly, so that now she was on her guard. She wouldn't let it happen again. But it had been nice of Lewis to be concerned about her.

It was with that thought uppermost in her mind that she eventually fell asleep. And when, much later, she awoke, it wasn't Jamie who woke her but the sound of a song thrush in the lilac tree outside her window.

In order to familiarise herself with every area of the surgical day unit Jo was asked to work on the ward attached to the unit the following morning. She found that instead of working with Pru who was in Theatre again that day she was to work with a staff nurse called Janet Luscombe.

Janet was brisk and very efficient and seemed to have little time for chit-chat. With a quick, satisfied glance around the empty ward with its two rows of neatly made beds she glanced at the list attached to the clipboard she was carrying. 'Would you call the first two patients from the day room, please?' she said, then added, 'They are Brenda Marshall for excision of a breast lump and Gwen Holt for varicose veins.'

Because she wasn't in Theatre that day Jo no longer wore the standard theatre greens and clogs. Instead, she was dressed in the blue and white check dress of a staff nurse together with black stockings and shoes.

The day room, when she arrived, was almost full—tense-looking people who looked up anxiously at her approach, listening for their names.

'Brenda Marshall?' she called, looking around the room.

A woman stood up on the far side, a tall woman with soft brown hair fashionably cut and wearing an expensive-looking sand-coloured suit.

'Brenda Marshall?' said Jo again.

The woman nodded. 'Yes, that's me,' she said.

'Would you come with me, please?' Jo paused, glanced around again and said, 'And is Gwen Holt here as well? Gwen Holt?'

'Oh, Lord, that's me.' A large woman, accompanied by two younger, but equally large women, an assortment of babies in buggies and what seemed to be dozens of shopping bags and supermarket carriers, struggled to her feet and stared at Jo. 'You want me as well, love?'

'Yes, please,' said Jo.

'Oh, well, I suppose we might as well get it over with,' said the large lady. 'I'll see you girls later. Mind you get here on time to pick me up. Byebye, my little loves.' Bending down, she planted a noisy kiss on each of the babies' faces, before joining Jo and Brenda Marshall.

'We're going to the ward now,' said Jo as they made their way down the corridor.

'What time are we going to have it done?' asked Gwen Holt.

'Very soon,' Jo replied. 'You two will be the first on the list.'

'You nervous, love?' Gwen turned to Brenda Marshall who hadn't as yet spoken a word.

'Well, it's not exactly a day out, is it?' said the younger woman coolly.

'Oh, I don't know,' said Gwen with a sniff as they reached the ward. 'It'll be rather nice to put my feet up for a while and have a decent sleep for once. What you in for?' she went on curiously.

When Brenda remained silent she added, 'I'm having me veins done. They've needed doing for years now. I was a hairdresser in my younger days—hard to believe now, isn't it?' She gave a short laugh. 'But it's true. All that standing, that's what done it, and having five kids—I don't suppose that helped either. I've been putting it off for years but it reached the stage I couldn't put it off no longer.

'"Gwen," my doctor says to me, "the time has come," and I reckon he were right an' all. They was getting pretty bad...' She trailed off as Jo turned to them.

'I'd like you to get undressed.' Jo drew the curtains around each of the first two beds. 'Put on a theatre gown and your own dressing-gown and slippers then I'll be back in a while to take some details.'

While the two patients were changing Jo collected their case histories and the letters from their GP's, together with urine pots, identity bands, thermometers and a sphygmomanometer, before making her way back to the beds. She went to Brenda Marshall first, drawing back the curtain and finding her sitting on the edge of the bed dressed in a cream satin dressing-gown with matching mules on her feet.

'Are you ready?' she asked.

'As ready as anyone could ever be for this,' the woman replied in a low tone, with a quick glance at the curtain which was all that separated her from Gwen Holt in the adjoining bed.

'I'd just like to check your details,' said Jo. 'Now, first of all, you haven't had anything to eat or drink since midnight, have you?'

When the patient confirmed this fact Jo carried straight on. 'So now I need to check your name and date of birth.' She entered each onto the plastic identity band, together with the patient's hospital number and the name of her consultant, which she then secured onto Brenda Marshall's wrist.

'Now temperature.' She popped the thermometer under Brenda's tongue. 'And while we're doing that, I'll check your blood pressure.' Pushing up the sleeve of the cream silk dressing-gown, Jo secured the cuff then put the stethoscope around her own neck while she squeezed the rubber pump.

'That's fine,' she said a moment later, after checking the reading. 'And so is that,' she added, after reading the thermometer.

'Now, I shall want you to do a specimen in there for me.' She handed over one of the small plastic urine pots. 'I know it's difficult to do to order so I'll leave the pot with you. The loos are at the end of the ward on the left.'

'You all right in there, love?' called Gwen's voice from behind the curtain.

Brenda's gaze met Jo's and she rolled her eyes, the gesture indicating she found her companion irritating beyond measure.

It was Jo who answered. 'We're fine, Mrs Holt. I'll be with you in a moment.'

'"Mrs Holt"? Good heavens, I thought me mother-in-law was in here for a moment,' said Gwen. 'Lord help us. Can't you call me Gwen? Everyone else does.'

Jo glanced up and just for the fraction of a second she could have sworn she saw Brenda Marshall's lips twitch. 'All right,' she called back. 'Gwen it is.

'The consultant will be along to see you soon.' Jo carried on talking, but quietly now, her remarks addressed to Brenda. 'And the anaesthetist. But first I need to ask you a few more questions.'

'All right.' Brenda Marshall nodded.

'The lump is on your left breast?'

'Yes.'

'Are you allergic to anything?'

'Not that I'm aware of.'

'No drugs? Penicillin or anything like that?'

'No, I don't think so.'

'Right,' Jo replied. 'Now, do you smoke?'

'No.'

'Do you have any of the following? Dentures, caps or crowns? Hearing aids or contact lenses?'

'I have two porcelain crowns.'

'Oh, I say, porcelain, eh?' called Gwen Holt from the next bed. 'Dead posh that. Mercury fillings, that's all I've got—dozens of them.'

'Gwen, please,' called Jo. 'Will you please not interrupt? I've told you I shall be with you shortly.'

'Sorry, I'm sure,' Gwen called back.

'How about your general health?' asked Jo, turning her attention to Brenda again. 'Any asthma, diabetes, epilepsy?'

'No.'

'Good. Now I need to ask how you will be getting home.'

'My husband will collect me.'

'That's fine, and he will be at home with you tonight?'

'Yes.'

'May I come in, please?' Jo, recognising the familiar voice, looked up sharply just as Lewis pulled back the curtain. His eyes immediately met hers and for some unknown reason she felt a warm little glow inside. Suddenly it was as if she had known him all her life—so intimate had they become in their domestic lives—instead of for just the few short days it had been in reality.

'This is Mr Gregson,' she explained to Brenda Marshall. 'He's the consultant anaesthetist and he will want to examine you. Mr Gregson this is Brenda Marshall. She's to have a lumpectomy this morning.'

'Hello, Mrs Marshall.' Lewis gave his rather solemn smile and for the first time, in response, Jo saw Brenda Marshall smile. 'Is there anything I need to know, Nurse?'

'Not really. Mrs Marshall is a non-smoker with no significant illnesses or allergies. She has two crowns.'

'Maybe you would like to point those out to me,' said Lewis quietly, 'just so that I'm aware of them.' As Brenda Marshall indicated the two crowned teeth, he nodded. 'Right, thank you. Now, I would just like to listen to your chest if I may.'

'Slip off your dressing-gown,' said Jo. Standing back, she watched as Lewis gently but thoroughly examined the patient. He looked every inch the consultant again in his dark suit, white shirt and his glasses, and for a moment it was hard to believe this was the same man she'd met on the landing that very morning dressed only in his towelling bathrobe with his hair still wet from the shower.

'That's fine,' he said at last, removing the stethoscope from his ears and letting it hang from his neck. 'Now, is there anything you want to ask me?'

'Will I be sick after the anaesthetic?' Brenda asked anxiously.

'You shouldn't be.' Lewis consulted her records. 'I see from your notes that you had an appendectomy in your teens,' he said after a moment. 'Were you sick after that anaesthetic?'

'Yes, I was.' Brenda nodded.

'In that case I'll give you an anti-emetic—that should prevent any nausea,' said Lewis. 'Now, is there anything else?'

'Not unless you have anything to prevent fear.'

'I wish I had,' said Lewis quietly. 'But try not to get too anxious.' As he spoke he stretched out his hand and gently touched Brenda's shoulder, the gesture both compassionate and reassuring. 'Staff Nurse will come down to the anaesthetic room with you,' he went on. 'I shall take over from her and then you will be in Mr Hughes's very capable hands. Has he been to see you yet this morning?'

'Not yet.' It was Jo who answered. 'But he'll be along in a moment.'

'If you have any questions about the operation itself or the procedure involved, you must ask him,' said Lewis. 'I'm sure he will do his best to put your mind at rest. When it's all over and you are back in the ward, I will come and see you again.'

As they moved out through the curtains into the ward again they were met by Janet Luscombe, who had brought a further two patients up from the day room. 'We have a Mrs Ryall in bed number three,' she said to Lewis. 'She's ready for you to see, Mr Gregson. And, Jo, if you would prepare Mrs Holt, please, while I prepare Mrs McNeill.'

Taking a deep breath, Jo slipped between the curtains that surrounded Gwen Holt.

'Hello, love.' Gwen was reading a TV magazine but she looked up and smiled as Jo came into the cubicle. 'My turn now, is it? Well, before you ask, yes, I am a smoker—although I've cut down recently. I only smoke about fifteen a day now. I've got a part plate, up the top here. I'm allergic to all metals except gold. I get very chesty and I'm always short of breath. I haven't had anything to eat or drink since midnight—nearly killed me that did, not having my early morning cuppa—and I don't wear contact lenses. Anything else you want to know?'

'Well, it sounds like you've covered most things,' said Jo, 'but can we take them one at a time, please? And slowly, starting with your name and date of birth.'

After completing the same routine that she had with Brenda Marshall, Jo was just filling in the last of Gwen Holt's details when she felt something touch her arm. Glancing down, she saw that it was Gwen herself who had touched her, and when she looked up the other woman put her finger to her lips then, with a quick glance at the curtain that divided her from Brenda, she mouthed. 'Poor soul.' At the same time she touched her own breast.

Jo was saved from showing any sort of reaction to this observation by the arrival of Lewis, who opened the curtain a couple of inches.

'Come in, Mr Gregson,' she said swiftly. 'We've just finished in here. Gwen, this is Mr Gregson.'

'Ah, so you're the one who's going to knock me out?' said Gwen, eyeing him up and down.

'Figuratively speaking, yes,' Lewis replied. 'Hello, Mrs Holt.'

'Mrs Holt prefers to be called Gwen,' said Jo.

'OK,' said Lewis easily. 'Gwen it is.'

'So what's your first name?' asked Gwen, still scrutinising him speculatively.

He looked a little surprised but replied, 'It's Lewis.'

'We've got a Lewis!' declared Gwen. 'My Mandy's boy is Lewis.'

'Is that so?' said Lewis, his expression inscrutable. 'Now, Nurse, is there anything I need to know about Gwen?'

'Where would you like her to start?' said Gwen Holt with a throaty laugh. 'I guess I must be every anaesthetist's nightmare. I'm overweight, I smoke, I'm chesty—you name it, I've got it or done it.'

'So, maybe we'd better start by examining you,' said Lewis, taking the stethoscope from around his neck as he perched on the side of the bed.

Throughout Lewis's examination Gwen kept up a non-stop stream of questions, observations and details of her life so that by the time he had finished there was very little about her that he didn't know.

'Like I say,' she said at the end, 'I'm probably going to be a nightmare for you.'

'I shall look on it as more of challenge,' said Lewis. 'But that isn't to say it wouldn't be better for you to try to lose some weight and to give up smoking altogether, so that if there's another time that we have to meet like this there won't be any talk of nightmares or challenges.'

'What do you mean—another time?' exclaimed Gwen indignantly. 'It took me long enough to agree to this time!'

'See you later, Gwen,' said Lewis. As he left the cubicle to move on down the line a smile played around his mouth.

'Isn't he lovely?' Gwen sighed. 'Don't you think so, Nurse?'

'Yes, he's very nice,' Jo agreed.

'Is he married?'

'No, he isn't married.'

'A good catch for somebody, then,' said Gwen as she pulled on her dressing-gown. Then, as Jo whipped back the curtains around both her bed and that of Brenda Marshall, she added, 'Are you married, Nurse?'

'No, Gwen, I'm not married,' said Jo.

'D'you hear that?' Gwen shot a sideways look at Brenda. 'Could have one of those hospital romances on our hands here. That gorgeous doctor is fancy-free and so is our little nurse here. They'd make a good pair, don't you think?'

'Actually, Gwen,' said Jo, 'Mr Gregson is a consultant.'

'Well, there you are, then. Even better,' said Gwen. 'And with a good job like that, he's probably rich as well. If I were you, Nurse, I'd get in there and snap him up quick—there can't be too many like him around. And he's nice with it. So many of the really dishy ones know it and underneath they're real so-and-sos but this one, well, you only have to look at his eyes to see what he's really like—'

'Mrs Holt!' said Jo sternly, only too aware that Lewis must be able to hear every word that was being said from the cubicle on the other side of Brenda Marshall.

'What?' Gwen looked up. 'What's wrong? Have I said something?'

'I think, Gwen, if you were to say just a little less,' said Jo.

'Oh, right,' said Gwen. 'Sorry. I know I talk too much. I just rabbit on sometimes. You'll just have to stop me when that happens. All right, love?' She turned to look at Brenda who, picking up a book, helplessly shook her head.

Play The *Lucky Hearts* Game

and get...

FREE BOOKS & a FREE GIFT... YOURS to KEEP!

Yes! I have scratched off the silver card. Please send me my **2 FREE BOOKS** and **FREE MYSTERY GIFT**. I understand that I am under no obligation to purchase any books as explained on the back of this card.

Scratch Here!
then look below to see what your cards get you.

370 HDL DC35   **170 HDL DC3U**

NAME   (PLEASE PRINT CLEARLY)

ADDRESS

APT.#   CITY

STATE/PROV.   ZIP/POSTAL CODE

The Harlequin Reader Service® — Here's how it works:

Accepting your 2 free books and gift places you under no obligation to buy anything. You may keep the books and gift and return the shipping statement marked "cancel." If you do not cancel, about a month later we'll send you 4 additional novels and bill you just $3.34 each in the U.S., or $3.74 each in Canada, plus 25¢ shipping & handling per book and applicable taxes if any.* That's the complete price and — compared to cover prices of $3.99 each in the U.S. and $4.50 each in Canada — it's quite a bargain! You may cancel at any time, but if you choose to continue, every month we'll send you 4 more books, which you may either purchase at the discount price or return to us and cancel your subscription.

*Terms and prices subject to change without notice. Sales tax applicable in N.Y. Canadian residents will be charged applicable provincial taxes and GST.

CHAPTER SEVEN

GRADUALLY all the patients for the morning's list were checked and prepared for surgery. After they had been examined by Lewis and seen by Mr Hughes, who was the consultant surgeon for that day, the two men took themselves off to the theatre changing rooms.

Jo and Janet stayed with the patients, answering any last-minute questions and offering reassurance. Brenda Marshall, especially, seemed to grow more nervous by the minute.

'You'll be all right, love,' called Gwen. 'Soon be all over now.'

'Well, it might be for you,' retorted Brenda, goaded at last into retaliation. 'You'll have your veins done, or whatever it is you're in for, and you'll go home, put your feet up for a couple of weeks and suffer no ill effects. I could lose a breast and have months of treatment ahead. I could have chemotherapy and lose my hair. I could be very sick—'

'You don't want to start talking like that, love.' Gwen sounded shocked. 'It's no good taking that attitude.'

'And what attitude do you suggest I take?' asked

113

Brenda sarcastically. 'Maybe I should be planning a big party—is that what you're saying? It's my fortieth birthday in a couple of months. Perhaps you think I should be writing out the invitations for a rave-up?'

Jo had been about to intervene, but something stopped her and she found herself holding her breath.

'Well, I don't see why not.' Gwen's reply was predictably down-to-earth. 'It'd do you a darn sight more good than lying there moaning about something that might never happen. For goodness' sake—you've got a lump. Millions of women get a lump. OK, it might be something nasty—in which case, hopefully they'll sort it out and, let's face it, that's why you're here—but there's a very good chance it's nothing at all, in which case you'll walk out of here as right as rain.

'Better than me, in actual fact. My poor old veins are all shot to pieces. No doubt it's all my own fault, but there it is. Mine is a fact—yours isn't, so there's no point in keeping going on about it until you're told otherwise.'

Jo's breath caught in her throat and she threw a fearful glance at Brenda to see how she was taking all this, but, far from the reaction she had feared, the woman seemed almost resigned to listening to what her companion was saying. Jo was saved from further anxiety by the arrival of an ODA from Theatre to tell them that they were ready for the first patient.

'That's you, Gwen,' said Jo briskly.

'Oh, Lord,' said Gwen. 'Here we go. Do I get a stretcher?'

'I think you'd probably be happier walking down, don't you?' said Jo. 'Don't worry, I'll come with you.'

As Gwen was about to leave the ward, unexpectedly Brenda Marshall called out to her. 'Good luck,' she said.

Gwen paused and looked back, a look of surprise on her face. 'Thanks, love,' she said. 'And you,' she added.

A few moments later as they approached the anaesthetic room Gwen threw Jo a wicked glance. 'Is this where I get to see that gorgeous anaesthetist again?'

'That's right, Gwen,' replied Jo with a smile. 'All this does have its compensations, you see.'

'He can put me to sleep any time he wants,' said Gwen with a chuckle.

Lewis himself met them at the door, dressed in theatre greens and wearing his cap and mask.

'You might have a mask on,' said Gwen, 'but there's no disguising who you are, not with those eyes.' She half turned to Jo. 'He looks like something out of *ER*, doesn't he?' she said with a sigh.

An ODA took over from Jo, helping Gwen onto the couch. Jo glanced at Lewis and their eyes met in the moment before she closed the door, and she murmured, 'I think you might have scored here, Mr Gregson.'

Because Jo's shift finished at lunchtime, she wasn't there when Lewis paid his second visit to the ward to see the patients before they were discharged. She'd seen both Gwen and Brenda come back from Theatre and had cared for them post-operatively, but both women had been still very sleepy and beyond conversation. It wasn't until early evening when Lewis returned from work that she was able to find out more.

The evening was warm and the children were playing in the garden. The two older ones were on the swing and the slide while Jo watched them from the patio with Jamie beside her in his buggy.

She hadn't heard Lewis arrive and he'd let himself into the house and come right through to the patio before she had realised he was there. It had been Francesca who had spotted him first.

'Uncle Lew!' she squealed. 'Look at me! Look at me!'

Jo had turned sharply to find him standing behind her. Her heart had turned over at the sight of him. Later, she convinced herself that it had simply been because she hadn't known he was there and he had made her jump, but at the time she was only aware that her pulse had started to race as she found herself wondering just how long he had been standing there, watching them all.

'Hi,' she said at last—she hoped casually—but feared it came out more as a nervous-sounding squeak. 'I didn't hear you come in.'

'A nice family scene,' he said, nodding towards the children. He sat down beside her and reached down to tickle Jamie's tummy.

'It's so warm out here—it seemed wrong to waste it by putting them to bed,' said Jo, turning away from him, suddenly confused by this new awareness of him. Instead, she stared down the garden past the children's play area to the mass of blossom on the fruit trees.

The silence grew between them, to such proportions that it became almost tangible. At last, in desperation, as she sought for something to say, she turned to him again and said the first thing that came into her head. 'How was Brenda Marshall?'

'She went home.' He nodded then, narrowing his eyes as he watched Alistair on the swing, he added, 'Actually, it was looking good. Edward didn't think the lump was malignant but, of course, only histology can confirm that.'

'Of course.' Jo nodded. 'And Gwen Holt?'

He chuckled. 'Gwen was Gwen until the bitter end. But, interestingly enough, when the chips were down a bit for Gwen—when she was feeling groggy after her op—it was Brenda who was there beside her. According to Janet Luscombe, they ended up the best of pals, even to the point of exchanging phone numbers because, as Gwen put it, she wants to know when Brenda gets the all-clear.'

'And if it isn't all clear, Gwen will be the first one to offer support,' observed Jo quietly.

'Exactly,' agreed Lewis. 'People are strange sometimes—it's very often the most unlikely ones who gel.'

They fell silent again, watching the children as they played, but each were busy with their own thoughts. At last Lewis yawned and stretched.

'Are you tired?' asked Jo.

'Not too bad.' He grinned. 'At least we got some sleep last night.' He looked down at Jamie. 'Make sure you keep up the good work tonight, young man, won't you? And it *is* Saturday tomorrow,' he added almost as a blissful afterthought.

'You're not talking lie-in, are you?' said Jo with a laugh.

'Heavens, no! Nothing as optimistic as that. But at least we don't have that mad scramble to get them off to school. One thing I will have to do, though, is a big shop at the supermarket. We're out of practically everything.'

'We'll go together,' said Jo.

'I can't expect your duties to extend to that,' Lewis replied.

'Nonsense,' Jo retorted. 'Two heads will be better

than one, I'm sure. Now, pleasant as this is sitting here, I guess I'd better start organising baths and bed.' Reluctantly she stood up. 'Alistair!' she called. 'Francesca! Come on, bath time.'

'Oh, no!' wailed Francesca.

'Not yet,' cried Alistair. 'Just ten more minutes.'

'Tell you what.' Lewis stood up. 'You see to Jamie. I'll sort those two little monsters out.'

'We're not monsters!' shrieked Francesca.

'Oh, yes, you are. And I'm a mega-monster.' Hunching his shoulders and pulling his jacket up over his head, Lewis began lumbering down the garden after the children, who shrieked afresh in delighted terror.

Jo watched them for a moment, laughing at Lewis's antics and the spontaneous response from the children, then with a little sigh she wheeled Jamie into the house and lifted him from his buggy. The baby nestled into her neck and impulsively she kissed the soft down on the top of his head. Momentarily she was reminded of Gwen Holt when she had kissed each of her grandchildren, before going for her op. Gwen may have exasperated staff and patients alike on the day unit but there was no denying her good nature or her capacity for love.

Jo was in a garden and she was watching a child on a swing. The swing was soaring higher and higher and she called out to the child to be careful. Then as the swing slowed down she saw that it was no longer a child on it but the very large, comfortable figure of Gwen Holt.

Somewhere a baby was crying. She talked to Gwen as she swung backwards and forwards, gently now, not soaring like before. The baby was still crying.

Jo opened her eyes. It was still dark. She turned her head and looked at the luminous numbers of her bedside clock. It was three-thirty. She had been dreaming. She turned over. The baby was still crying. So that hadn't been in the dream. She sat up and listened. It was Jamie who was crying.

Slipping out of bed and not even stopping to put a wrap over her nightshirt, Jo padded barefoot to the door which once again she had left ajar. The light which they left on for the children was burning dimly on the landing and she could see the glow of the nightlight through the partly open door in Jamie's room.

As she pushed the nursery door fully open she saw Lewis, standing at the chest of drawers. He was wearing only a pair of boxer shorts and was struggling to change Jamie's nappy. The baby was lying on his plastic changing mat and was kicking furiously, his small fists waving in the air as his cries pierced the silence of the night.

'Sorry,' mumbled Jo as she struggled through the

mists of sleep. 'You still seem to hear him before I do. Can I help?'

'It's OK, I think we're nearly there,' muttered Lewis as he battled with baby wipes. 'He seems very unhappy about something.'

'I expect it's his teeth,' said Jo. 'His little face was rather flushed this evening. I'll go and get him a drink.' Leaving Lewis to cope with the adhesive strips on the disposable nappy, she fumbled her way out onto the landing and down the stairs to the kitchen where she poured cooled, ready-boiled water into one of Jamie's sterilised bottles.

Moments later she was back in the nursery where she found Lewis nursing Jamie against his shoulder. He took the bottle from her and settled the baby into the crook of his arm. For the next few moments the only sound in the nursery was that of faint gulps as the baby swallowed the water.

'Becky said she keeps Calpol in the bathroom cabinet,' Lewis said at last. 'Maybe we should give him some?'

'Yes, maybe,' Jo replied. 'What do you think?'

'Well, I can't see it would do any harm and it might help to settle him down. Here, he's finished his water—you burp him and I'll go and fetch the Calpol.'

'All right.' Carefully Jo took the baby from Lewis's arms, and as she did so her bare skin touched his chest. It was only later when she thought about it that it seemed unbelievable that they should have been there like that in the middle of the night, he in his underpants and she in her nightshirt, but at the time the only important thing was that they try to pacify the fretful baby.

At last Jamie settled, his eyelids slowly closed and Jo placed him back in his cot. Together, she and Lewis tiptoed out of the nursery. On the landing Jo had to fight a sudden uncontrollable impulse to giggle and had to press her hand to her mouth.

'What is it?' Lewis had been about to go back to his own room but he must have seen the expression on her face for he stopped and peered closely at her in the half-light. 'What's the matter?'

'Nothing,' she whispered. 'It's silly really, but I just thought—there's you a consultant and me a staff nurse, and neither of us was really sure whether or not to give a baby a spoonful of Calpol.'

Lewis must have seen the funny side of the situation for he, too, smiled, albeit a weary smile. 'Goodness knows how some of these young parents manage,' he said. 'Anyway, I'm back to my bed and I suggest you do the same.' He paused, then briefly reached out his hand and touched her arm. 'Thanks for your help, Jo.'

'That's OK.' She smiled. 'See you later.'

She fell asleep again instantly as soon as her head touched the pillow and this time her sleep was deep and dreamless.

The sound of the telephone woke her. She sat up with a start and was about to get up to answer it when it stopped ringing. She listened, heard the sound of Lewis's voice and guessed he had answered it. No doubt it was the hospital, wanting him for another emergency. She sank back onto her pillow. It was only a quarter to seven, with a bit of luck she might manage another fifteen minutes or so of sleep before the children awoke.

'Jo! Jo! Wake up. Look at us. We've brought your breakfast.'

Jo opened her eyes. Francesca was peering down at her, her little face only inches from her own. Startled, Jo struggled to sit up, then realised that Alistair was behind Francesca and behind both of them stood Lewis with a tray in his hands. He was wearing his towelling bathrobe and was looking rather embarrassed.

'We brought you orange juice and toast,' said Francesca.

'And coffee,' said Alistair.

'And a flower,' added Francesca. 'Daddy brings a rose for Mummy but I couldn't find any roses so I picked a bluebell 'cos I'm going to be a bluebell at dancing.'

Sure enough, in one corner of the tray a single bluebell stood in a jam jar filled with water. 'Well this is very kind of you,' said Jo, 'but you really didn't have to, you know.'

'Yes, we did,' said Francesca solemnly. 'Daddy always lets us do it for Mummy on Saturday mornings when he's at home.'

'Which isn't really very often,' said Alistair. 'So we thought as we are all here this morning we would bring your breakfast instead.'

'Hope you don't mind,' said Lewis helplessly, his eyes meeting hers.

'No, of course not,' said Jo, pushing the hair out of her eyes. 'What about you?' she said, peering at the tray as he set it down on the bedside table. 'Have you got anything?'

'I've got a cup of coffee,' Lewis replied.

'When we do this for Mummy she lets us all get into bed with her,' said Francesca hopefully.

Jo only hesitated for a moment, then she lifted back one corner of her covers. 'Come on,' she said. 'And you, Alistair.'

The children needed no second bidding, settling themselves down on either side of Jo.

'And you, Uncle Lew,' said Francesca, looking up at Lewis. 'There's plenty of room for you as well.'

'I think, actually, if you don't mind,' said Lewis gravely, 'I'll just sit here on the edge of the bed and drink my coffee. We don't want any accidents with hot drinks, do we?'

That seemed to satisfy the children who proceeded

to help Jo to polish off her toast which someone had thoughtfully cut into soldiers and spread with Marmite.

'Is Jamie awake yet?' asked Jo weakly, refusing either to face up to the incongruity of the situation or to meet Lewis's gaze.

'No,' said Alistair. 'He was still asleep.'

'He was naughty in the night,' announced Francesca with obvious relish.

'Tell us about it.' Lewis pulled a face. 'We were there.'

'Not really naughty,' said Jo. 'His teeth were playing him up, poor little chap.'

'He hasn't got many teeth yet,' declared Alistair.

'That's why they were playing him up,' said Lewis.

'Did I hear the phone just now?' Jo looked from one to another of them.

'Yes,' said Francesca, popping another piece of toast into her mouth. 'It was Mummy. I said hello to her. She said hello to me and her voice sounded really funny—like she was crying or something.'

Jo threw Lewis a quick glance.

'It's OK,' he said quickly, obviously reading the question in her eyes. 'Apparently the new treatment has arrived and they started it last night.'

'Why do you think Mummy was talking funny?' asked Francesca.

'Probably because she's missing you...and Alistair...and Jamie,' said Lewis.

Both children seemed to consider this then, changing the subject with a speed that almost took Jo's breath away, Francesca went on, 'You're going out tonight, aren't you, Jo?'

'And how did you know that?' asked Jo with a sideways glance at the little girl.

It was Alistair, however, who answered because by then Francesca had her mouth full of toast again. 'Uncle Lew told us,' he said.

'Oh,' said Jo. 'I see. Well, yes, that's right. As it happens, I am going out.'

Francesca swallowed. 'Uncle Lew said you had a lovely dress to wear. Can I see it?'

'I expect so...' Jo, aware suddenly that Lewis was watching her, wished that she hadn't just woken up and that her hair wasn't all over the place.

'I want you to come in and see me before you go,' Francesca went on. 'Mummy does that when she and Daddy are going out. She always lets me see what she's wearing.'

'All right,' Jo agreed.

'Where are you going?' asked Alistair suddenly. He had been turning the pages of a book he had brought into the bedroom with him and hadn't appeared to be taking any notice of the conversation.

'To a disco at the club at the hospital,' Jo replied.

'Who are you going with?' Suddenly Alistair seemed to want to know everything.

'One of the doctors has asked me to go with him,' said Jo, carefully avoiding Lewis's eye.

'Uncle Lew is a doctor,' said Francesca. 'Is it Uncle Lew you're going with?'

'No,' said Jo. 'It isn't Uncle Lew. It's another doctor.'

'What's his name?' demanded Francesca.

'His name is Dr Jacobs,' said Jo.

'I think that's a silly name,' said Francesca with a pout. 'When Mummy goes out she goes with Daddy. I think you should go out with Uncle Lew, not with silly Dr Jacobs...silly Dr Jacobs...silly Dr Jacobs,' she chanted, bouncing up and down on the bed.

'That's quite enough, Francesca,' said Lewis sternly. 'Keep still or you'll upset Jo's coffee.'

'And you've woken Jamie up,' declared Alistair disapprovingly as the sounds of the baby could be heard coming from the nursery.

'I'll go—' Jo began, but Lewis put out a hand to restrain her.

'No,' he said, 'finish your breakfast. Alistair, you and Francesca go and talk to Jamie. I'll be along in a moment.'

As the children scrambled off the bed and disappeared out of the room, Lewis gave Jo a rueful look. 'Sorry about all this enforced happy-family bit,' he said lightly. 'It somehow seemed easier to go along with what the children wanted to do.'

'Don't worry about it, honestly,' said Jo quickly. 'It doesn't matter, really it doesn't. To tell you the truth, I've actually quite enjoyed it,' she admitted.

'God knows what Francesca's nursery teacher will make of it when she tells them we were all in bed together on Saturday morning.'

'But we weren't,' protested Jo. 'At least, you weren't actually in the bed...'

'Maybe not,' said Lewis wryly, 'but you can bet that's what Francesca will tell her. Anyway...' he drained his mug then stood up '...I'll leave you in peace now. Thanks for going along with the charade.'

And that's all it was, thought Jo as Lewis went out of her room—a charade. But she was forced to admit it had been a very pleasant charade. In fact, if she really thought about it, the whole thing was proving to be more pleasant than she had ever dreamed possible, in spite of the hard work and broken sleep. There was something very pleasurable about the unconditional love one received from small children and, even though she was more reluctant to admit it, there was also something rather pleasant about sharing it all with Lewis Gregson—the sharing and planning of it all, the mutual pride in the children, the midnight conspiracy and, last but by no means least, having him sit on her bed as she ate her breakfast.

The rest of the day was as action-filled as ever, with the proposed trip to the supermarket, followed by lunch then an outing to the park to feed the ducks. After tea and baths Lewis took over the story session while Jo went to get ready for her night out.

When Marcus had first asked her to go to the Seventies night with him she had been pleased and had imagined that as the time grew closer she would be so looking forward to it that she would be counting the hours. The reality was actually quite different for she'd been so busy that she'd hardly had time to even think about the forthcoming evening, and even when she was getting ready and lying in a scented bath she felt so tired that it would have taken very little to persuade her to change her mind and settle for a quiet night in.

Even stepping into the green chiffon dress and spraying herself with her favourite perfume did little to restore her spirits. She only hoped she didn't look as weary as she felt.

'Oh, Jo, you look lovely,' breathed Francesca a little later when Jo made the promised visit to the little girl's room. And as Jo bent down to give her a goodnight kiss she said, 'You smell just like Mummy.'

Lewis was still reading to Alistair as Jo paused in the boy's bedroom doorway. They both looked up and Jo saw a strange expression cross Lewis's features—the same expression she'd seen when she'd first tried on the green dress.

'Have a good time,' he said softly.

At that moment she would have given anything in the world not to be going out. She'd much rather have been simply getting the children settled then going downstairs with Lewis, perhaps to share a glass of wine, supper and a chat before bed. 'Don't wait up,' she heard herself say. 'I may be late.'

'I'll leave the hall light on.'

'All right. Goodnight Alistair.'

'Night, Jo. You look nice,' the little boy murmured sleepily.

At that moment the doorbell sounded. 'That'll be Marcus,' said Jo. 'I must go.' Suddenly she found it impossible to meet Lewis's gaze and instead she fled. She was halfway down the stairs when Jamie began to cry. She stopped and looked up anxiously. Lewis came out of Alistair's room and paused on the landing, looking over the bannisters at her.

'It's all right,' he said. 'I'll see to him. You go on.'

'But…what if it's his teeth playing him up again?'

'Then I'll give him Calpol,' said Lewis calmly. 'No messing about tonight.' The doorbell sounded for the second time. 'Go on,' he said. 'Don't keep him waiting.'

Swallowing the lump that had unexpectedly risen in her throat, Jo went on slowly down the stairs and opened the front door.

CHAPTER EIGHT

FOR one moment Jo hardly recognised Marcus Jacobs. With his dark hair curled, sporting a false black moustache and wearing a frilly shirt and flared deep purple trousers, he looked as far removed as it was possible to be from his usual image.

'Did they really dress like this in the Seventies?' Jo spluttered as she climbed into the passenger seat of Marcus's VW.

'I can remember my dad in flared trousers just like this,' said Marcus with a grin, 'and I can vaguely recall my mum having an accident with a pair of platform shoes.' He paused and threw her a glance. 'I must say you look sensational in that dress.'

'Thanks,' she replied, feeling the colour flood her face at the look in his eyes. 'Aren't you meant to be some television detective or other?' she added in an attempt to divert the conversation away from herself. 'I can't remember his name.'

'That's right.' Marcus nodded. 'It's Jason King, actually.'

'Oh, yes. That's right.' Jo laughed. 'I wasn't allowed to stay up to watch that programme. Mum said it was too late...and I dare say she thought it was too violent as well. How times have changed!'

'This is some place you have here.' Marcus glanced back at the house as he turned the key in the ignition.

'It isn't mine,' said Jo hastily. 'I'm only living here temporarily while I'm looking after the children.'

'Oh, yes.' Marcus let out the clutch and they roared away. 'Lewis Gregson's brood.'

'They aren't his children,' said Jo quickly. 'They're his sister's. I'm just helping out for a while, that's all.' She still didn't want Marcus to know that Lewis himself was also living at the house. She wasn't sure why she didn't want him to know—she just had the feeling it would complicate matters and involve a lot of explanations.

When they reached the hospital social club it was to find that many others had already arrived. Amidst much hilarity they discovered at least two other Jason King look-alikes, two white-suited Elvis Presleys, one very large, kaftan-clad Demis Roussos, a motley crew of flower-power hippies, complete with sandals, beads and flowing robes, and the odd BeeGee or two.

After greeting several fellow members of staff, Marcus steered Jo to a table in an intimate little alcove on the far side of the dance floor. Leaving her there, he went off to the bar to order their drinks.

'You look fab in that dress!'

Jo looked up quickly to find Pru grinning down at her. 'I saw it myself when I went to get mine,' Pru went on, 'I would have liked it but there was no way I was going to squeeze *my* bum into it.'

'But you look great,' said Jo, eyeing her friend up and down. Pru was clad in a saffron-coloured kaftan, complete with a long blonde wig and an assortment of bangles, beads, necklaces and ankle chains.

'He looks more dangerous than ever in that get-up,' muttered Pru, turning to look at Marcus as he stood at the bar.

'Who are you with?' asked Jo, looking round.

'No one in particular.' Pru shrugged.

'Then you must join us,' said Jo firmly.

'Marcus won't like that.'

'Of course he will. Don't be silly. He won't mind,' said Jo, making room for Pru on the seat beside her.

'So where's the hunky Lewis tonight?' asked Pru, looking round.

'He's babysitting,' said Jo, and was surprised to find that at the mention of Lewis's name she felt an inexplicable pang, almost of regret—regret that Lewis wasn't there with them.

Which was crazy really, she told herself sharply. She could be with Lewis all the time, not only at work but at home as well. She should be making the most of this break, and after all Marcus was her date that night, not Lewis. Most of the female staff on the day unit, if not of the whole hospital, would no doubt have given their eye teeth for a date with Marcus Jacobs, so she might as well enjoy the experience even if she did still feel strange at what was her first real date since Simon.

At that moment Marcus returned from the bar with their drinks, and as he set them down on the table he gave Pru a sharp look.

'I said Pru could join us,' said Jo quickly. 'I knew you wouldn't mind.'

Marcus didn't answer and Jo found herself wondering if perhaps Pru had been right after all and that he did mind. She didn't, however, have time to wonder any further for at that moment the DJ put on a popular Abba hit from the Seventies and people began to flock onto the dance floor in droves.

Jo felt Marcus's hand beneath her elbow as he guided her forward, and as people surged around them for the time being they lost sight of Pru.

'Did you arrange for her to join us?' asked Marcus as he drew Jo into his arms.

'Who, Pru?' said Jo. 'No, not really. It was just that she was alone and I thought she might like to sit with us, that's all. I like Pru,' she added as an afterthought. 'She's been kind to me since I arrived at St Theresa's.'

When Marcus remained silent she moved her head so that she could look into his face. 'Don't you like her?' she asked.

'She's OK.' He shrugged. 'Not really my cup of tea.'

'I'm sorry if you think I did wrong—' she began stiffly.

'Of course you didn't do wrong. It's just that...' He tightened his grip on her. 'I don't want to share you with anyone tonight. I want you all to myself.' He drew her even closer as he spoke, so close that his cheek rubbed against her own.

It was a small, almost insignificant incident, but somehow it left Jo feeling vaguely uneasy.

As the evening moved on the music went from one vintage hit to another and the fun became fast and furious. Marcus was very attentive, so attentive as to be bordering almost on the possessive. He danced only with Jo, and while she found his attentions to some extent flattering she would also quite have liked to dance with some of the other members of staff.

Marcus didn't even dance with Pru. Indeed, he hardly spoke to her, something which Jo found increasingly embarrassing—so much so that as The Three Degrees were asking someone when they would see them again, she felt an overwhelming sense of relief as Gary Kent, one of the ODAs, came across and took Pru off to the dance floor.

'Shall we sit this one out?' said Marcus, moving closer to Jo in the alcove.

'Yes, all right.' She nodded, glad for the moment of the respite and the chance to cool down.

'You know something?' Marcus took her hand,

lifted it to his lips, planted a kiss on the palm then folded her fingers over as if capturing it. 'You and I look really good together, Jo. I have the feeling we could really go places.'

'Is that a fact?' Jo nearly laughed, only just stopping herself, unable to decide whether he was joking or serious. The chat-up line seemed just too corny to be true. Marcus, however, didn't seem in any way deterred, continuing with more of the same.

'I felt it the moment I set eyes on you,' he murmured against her ear. 'And I really think we should do something about getting to know each other a whole lot better.'

As he spoke his arm, which had been resting along the back of the seat, slid across her shoulders and he began playing with her hair, letting it slip through his fingers. Suddenly his approach changed, shifting from being light-hearted, even corny, to something altogether different.

Jo stiffened. She didn't usually react in this way when a handsome man paid her attention. Maybe she was more vulnerable than she'd thought after Simon but, whatever it was, she knew she wasn't happy to have Marcus touching her in this way. She tried to pull away from him and move along the seat, but his response was simply to move closer. This time, instead of just playing with her hair, he began to caress her cheek with his thumb.

That was enough for Jo and she slid right out of the alcove and stood up.

'Where're you going?' Marcus looked startled as if he was totally unused to such a reaction.

'To the loo,' said Jo swiftly. 'Won't be long.' Somehow she managed to fight her way through the crowd and into the comparative quiet and coolness of the foyer.

After cooling her cheeks with cold water and repairing her make-up, Jo took a long look at herself in the mirror above the washbasins. Then, squaring her shoulders, she took a deep breath and prepared to enter the fray again. She wished now she had insisted on bringing her own car when Marcus had said he would pick her up. But it was too late now and she knew she would just have to make the best of it.

She was about to leave the Ladies when two young women came in, chattering to each other.

'You found a babysitter, then?' said one.

'Yes. I didn't think I was going to be able to come at first,' said the other. 'Sasha is teething and I don't like to leave her with our usual babysitter when she's like that. She gets so fretful. But then my mum offered to have her...'

Jo didn't hear any more because by then the heavy door had swung to behind her and she was in the foyer once more. She didn't, however, go straight back to the dance floor. The woman's words somehow kept reverberating in her head. Teething. Babies.

Fretful. Jamie was teething, he got fretful. Had been fretful the night before.

Images flooded her mind—of Lewis holding the baby against his chest, of Francesca and Alistair asleep in their beds, of the lovely, rambling old house in Mowbery Avenue—and quite suddenly that was where she wanted to be, back there with them, not in this noisy, smoky club, being pawed by some man she hardly knew who seemed to think it was somehow his right to do exactly as he wanted simply because he had brought her here for the evening.

On a sudden impulse she crossed the foyer to the phone booth in the far corner, scrambled in her bag for some loose change, then dialled the Cunningham's's number. Lewis answered on the fourth ring. The sound of his voice was as comforting as a warm fireside on a cold day.

'Hello, Lewis?' she said.

'Yes, Jo?' He sounded surprised.

'Yes.' Suddenly she didn't know what to say.

'Is everything all right?' he said, and at the obvious note of concern in his voice Jo felt her throat tighten with emotion.

'Yes. Yes,' she said quickly. 'Everything is fine. Noisy, but fine. I…er…I just thought I'd ring to see if Jamie is all right.'

'Yes, he is. Haven't had a cheep out of him—yet.'

'Oh, that's good. I just thought you might be having problems with him, that's all…' She trailed off, not knowing what else to say. 'Are—are the other two all right?' she said at last.

'Yes. Both asleep.'

'Oh, good.' Once again she longed to be there with them all. The children asleep upstairs, and she and Lewis...

She clutched the phone more tightly. 'I'd better go,' she said at last.

'Yes, all right. I'll see you later.' He paused while Jo continued to clutch the receiver, not knowing what else to say.

'Jo?' he said at last.

'Yes?' she said.

'Are you sure you're all right?'

'Yes, Lewis. Of course. I'm fine. Bye.' She replaced the receiver and for a long moment simply stood there, staring at the phone. Then, turning, she walked slowly back into the crowded club. Wending her way back through the dancers, she reached the alcove where Marcus was sitting.

'Oh, there you are,' he said, eyeing her up and down. 'I was beginning to wonder where you had got to.'

Jo suddenly, unreasonably almost, wanted to ask if he'd been in the least bit concerned about the fact that she had been so long, but before she even had the chance to phrase the question Pru came back to the table with Gary Kent.

'Can I get you guys a drink?' asked Gary pleasantly.

'No, it's OK, I was about to get some,' said Marcus. As he stood up he added, 'Save your money—you'll be short after tonight.' He grinned and Gary glanced at Jo. Then he, too, grinned and winked before he sat down next to Pru.

Jo had no idea what they were talking about but, whatever it was, it seemed to add to the sense of unease that she'd had almost from the start of the evening. Suddenly she wanted to talk to Pru, to tell her that she wasn't happy with the situation and that she was thinking of getting a cab and going home. But Pru seemed to be getting on very well with Gary, and before Jo could say anything the young ODA had whisked her away onto the floor as the gravelly tones of Barry White put everyone in a sensuous mood.

Marcus came back to the table, set down the tray of drinks and, without even asking, took Jo's hands and pulled her to her feet. Drawing her onto the dance floor, immediately he enfolded her in his arms and began nuzzling her neck and nibbling at her earlobe.

The lights had dimmed, to such an extent that it was practically impossible to discern any of the closely entwined couples who moved and swayed alongside them, so it seemed to Jo a pretty fair bet that those other couples could see little or nothing of herself and Marcus.

That Marcus himself was also only too aware of this became more than obvious when, taking full advantage of the situation, his hands began to roam. At first he confined their movement to Jo's back, running them from her shoulders to her waist, but she soon got the distinct impression that he wouldn't be content with that. Sure enough, as Barry White continued to growl his way through his song, she felt Marcus begin to stroke her hips then, more daringly, her buttocks. She flinched at that and tried to pull away, but he merely held her even closer, the hardness of his body leaving no doubt as to his state of arousal.

'I've got an idea,' he murmured smoothly against her hair. 'I guess there's not much point us going back to your place for coffee when this is over—not with a houseful of kids there—so how about we go to my place?'

'I don't think so, Marcus,' she replied tightly.

'Oh, you're going to play hard to get—this is getting better and better. I love women who do that. Somehow it seems to add to the excitement.' As he spoke he nuzzled her neck again.

'No, Marcus, you misunderstand. I'm not playing hard to get,' said Jo. 'I'm saying no.'

'An ice maiden?' he muttered. 'Even better.' Moving his hands rapidly, so rapidly that it almost took Jo's breath away, he covered her breasts, his fingers and thumbs seeking then pinching her nipples through the soft fabric of her dress.

She gasped at his audacity and the roughness of his movement.

'Now, tell me you don't like that,' he said.

In one sudden movement, which took him completely unawares, she jerked away from him, turned and fled back to their table where she grabbed her bag, before pushing her way through the mass of gyrating bodies to the exit. She had no idea whether Marcus attempted to follow her or whether he even called out. She only knew she had to get away from him and as quickly as possible.

She was just struggling into her jacket in the foyer and wondering if there were any numbers of local cab firms listed in the phone booth when Pru suddenly appeared at her elbow.

'Jo?' she said. 'What is it?'

'I'm going home,' said Jo.

'I'll take you,' said Pru unhesitatingly.

'No,' Jo replied quickly. 'I wouldn't dream of dragging you away. I'll get a cab.'

'You won't be dragging me away from anything, I assure you.' Pru pulled off the blonde wig as she spoke. 'Come on, my car's in the car park and you needn't worry—I've been drinking mineral water all evening.'

Together they hurried from the club, and to Jo's relief there was no further sign of Marcus.

'I'm sorry about this,' said Jo as she climbed into the passenger seat of Pru's car.

'Don't be,' said Pru. 'There's no need, believe me. I take it Marcus was coming on strong?'

Jo nodded. 'Something like that. I think he thought because he'd paid for my ticket he had exclusive rights to do as he pleased.'

'Sounds like Marcus,' said Pru grimly as she reversed the car out of its space. 'Running true to form, I would say. In fact, I was expecting it—that's why I hung around. I thought you might be glad of an escape route.'

'Really?' Jo turned her head and looked at Pru in amazement.

'I've been there, Jo. I know,' said Pru ruefully.

'What, with Marcus?'

'Yes,' said Pru quietly. By this time they were approaching the main Queensbury road.

'I didn't know,' said Jo. 'I wish you'd said.'

'I couldn't,' Pru replied. 'Not really. I did try to warn you but I thought if I said too much it would just sound like sour grapes. Besides, it was a long time ago.'

'So are you saying he did the same to you?'

'There was a bit more to it than that,' Pru replied. 'I wasn't quite as sensible as you, Jo. And I hate to admit it but, yes, I got hurt...'

'Oh, Pru, I'm sorry. I do wish I'd known.' She paused as Pru negotiated the large roundabout and took the exit for the out-of-town route. 'So have there been others? With Marcus, I mean?'

'Yes, Jo. Many, many others.'

'Oh, God!' said Jo. 'I suppose everyone else knows what he's like and I dare say they were all looking at me and assuming I was about to become another notch on his bedpost...'

'Only you haven't...have you?' said Pru with a low chuckle. 'Believe me, word will soon get round that you walked out on him. There aren't too many that do that right at the beginning, not with Marcus Jacobs.'

'So what was all that with Gary Kent?' asked Jo.

'Marcus will have had a bet with Gary,' Pru replied.

'A bet?' said Jo faintly.

'Yes. That he would get you into bed before the end of the night—it's what they do, Jo.'

'Oh, for pity's sake!' said Jo angrily. 'Who does he think he is, God's gift to women?'

'Yes, unfortunately, I think he does think just that,' Pru replied as she turned the car into Mowbery Avenue. 'I guess he thinks he's utterly irresistible.'

'You seemed to be getting on rather well with Gary Kent.'

'Not really.' Pru shrugged then shook her head. 'Gary's all right but he's nearly as bad as Marcus when it comes to women and scoring points. Honestly, Jo, I've come to the conclusion that men are all the same, and I guess you must be feeling that as well what with your last disastrous affair with—what was his name?'

'Simon.'

'Yes, Simon, and now this…' Pru leaned forward and peered through the windscreen. 'Now, where's the house? This one? Right.' She brought the car to a halt outside Chilterns. The hall light was burning, clearly visible in the stained-glass fanlight above the front door.

'Lewis isn't like that,' said Jo.

'Lewis Gregson?' Pru turned to look at her in the darkness. 'How do you know?'

'I just do, that's all,' said Jo.

They were silent for a while, and it was as if Pru was waiting for Jo to elaborate in some way on what she had just said.

'He's never taken advantage of me once,' Jo said at last. 'Not once, either of me or of the situation. And, heaven knows, there's been opportunity enough. I shudder to think what Marcus Jacobs would have done in the same sort of situations.'

'What situations?' asked Pru.

Jo took a deep breath. 'Everything, really. Living in the same house, sharing meals…shopping, looking after the children. Take this morning, for example…'

'So, what happened this morning?'

'Well, apparently,' said Jo, 'when their father is at home on a Saturday morning the children always take breakfast to their mother in bed.'

'Yes?' said Pru with obvious interest. 'Go on.'

'Well, they wanted to do the same for me. So they got Lewis to help. That's all really…' She trailed off.

Pru, however, wasn't prepared to leave it there. 'You mean,' she said, 'that there's you in bed, and Lewis comes in with the children, who are pretending that you are their mother, complete with your breakfast on a tray. You're going to tell me in a minute there was there a red rose on the tray.' There was amusement in Pru's voice now.

'Er…'

'You mean there was?' The expression on Pru's face was almost comical.

'Not exactly,' Jo replied. 'It was a bluebell actually. There weren't any roses in bloom.'

'So, what happened?' With a chuckle Pru seemed to settle herself more comfortably in her seat.

'What do you mean, what happened?' Jo was beginning to wish she hadn't started this conversation. She had the feeling that whatever she said it might be horribly misconstrued.

'Well, presumably, if the children were pretending you were their mother,' said Pru, 'then by the same token they were also pretending Lewis Gregson was their father. Am I correct?'

'Well, yes, sort of, I suppose…' said Jo helplessly.

'In which case that would make you and he an item…'

'Oh, hardly. Come on, Pru,' protested Jo. She was laughing now.

'Is that so improbable?' asked Pru. 'After all, it's pretty obvious your mind was working along those lines.'

'Whatever do you mean?' demanded Jo indignantly, half turning to stare at Pru in the darkness.

'Well, just now,' Pru went on, 'when I was about to tar all men with the same brush as the one I used for Marcus Jacobs and your ex—Simon—I seem to recall you rushed speedily to Lewis Gregson's defence. Now, I ask myself, if your mind wasn't working along those lines, why in the world would you have felt the need to do such a thing?'

CHAPTER NINE

LEWIS was in the sitting room when Jo let herself into the house. The television was on but she suspected he wasn't really watching it as he flicked it off via the remote control as soon as she entered the room.

'Hello,' he said. 'You're early. I didn't expect you for ages yet.'

'I was tired,' said Jo. She tried to keep her voice casual but was amazed by the overwhelming feeling of relief which had flooded over her. She didn't want Lewis to know the real reason she had left the club early. Telling Pru, that was one thing. Telling Lewis, that was something else altogether. Somehow she had the feeling that things might be very uncomfortable indeed for Marcus Jacobs if Lewis Gregson got to hear of his behaviour.

'So, wasn't it very good, then?' His eyes narrowed slightly.

'It wasn't bad.' She shrugged.

'Where's Jacobs?' He looked past her to the open door as if he expected Marcus Jacobs to be standing there. 'Didn't he bring you home?'

'No, actually, Pru brought me home,' said Jo lightly.

'Pru?' Lewis frowned. 'What was wrong with Jacobs, for God's sake? Too much to drink, I presume?'

Jo gave a noncommittal little shrug, letting him believe that if he wanted to. It was far easier than explaining the truth.

'All quiet upstairs?' she said.

He nodded. 'Yes.'

'Well, I guess I'd better get to bed just in case the peace doesn't last,' she said, moving to the door.

'Oh, there was one other thing,' he said. 'Just after you phoned Becky rang. Apparently there has been a dramatic improvement in David's condition since they started the new treatment.'

'That's wonderful,' she said.

'She said if the improvement continues and there are no further setbacks they are talking of moving him in less than a week's time.'

She had been about to go out into the hall but she paused, one hand on the doorhandle. 'When you say move him, what exactly do you mean?'

'Airlift him to a UK hospital.'

'That's marvellous,' she said faintly.

'At least Becky will be able to come home. Even if he's in a London hospital she'll be able to visit him from here. Which means, of course, our responsibilities will be at an end.'

'Yes, I suppose it does,' she replied. She should have felt something at the prospect—relief, elation maybe—so why was it, as she walked out into the hall with Lewis behind her, that all she was conscious of was a sense of depression?

Slowly she began to climb the stairs, one hand on the bannisters, the hem of the green chiffon dress trailing each stair. Suddenly she felt Lewis's hand cover hers on the bannister. She stopped and looked down at him.

'I couldn't have done it without you, Jo,' he said.

'You were doing all right before I came,' she said quietly.

'Maybe, but I wouldn't have been able to keep working. It was impossible. I was almost at the end of my tether when you came along.'

His touch was warm, his fingers strong, so different from the feel of Marcus's hands on her.

'I'll always be grateful to you,' he added.

Gratitude. Was that all it was? Was that all he felt towards her? Briefly she allowed her eyes to meet his.

'Goodnight, Jo,' he said softly.

'Goodnight, Lewis,' she replied.

Gratitude, she told herself again as she prepared for bed. But what else could there be? What else could she expect? Nothing, surely. Lewis was, in effect, her employer, albeit for such a brief time—nothing more, nothing less.

But what was it that Pru had been suggesting? She

had seized on the fact that Jo had leapt to Lewis's defence when Pru had suggested that he was the same as all men. But she had felt compelled to do that. There was no way that she could have Lewis compared with the likes of Simon or the odious Marcus Jacobs—there simply wasn't any comparison between them and the man she had seen at work in the theatre or caring for the Cunningham children.

She could still hardly believe how wrong she had been about Marcus, and she shuddered afresh as she recalled the evening and what might have happened had she allowed him to drive her home or, even worse, if he had taken her back to his flat.

In a way it was a shame that this, her first attempt at a date since Simon, had been such a disaster for it certainly had done little to restore her confidence.

She frowned as she lay in the darkness. What was it Marcus had said? He had called her an ice maiden. Was there any truth in that? Had she become frigid? Had that been a legacy of Simon's betrayal? How terrible if that were true. But she certainly hadn't been frigid before that, and surely with the right man...but who would that man be? Would she ever be able to trust again?

She sighed and turned over. She knew she really ought to try to get some sleep. There was no knowing if Jamie would wake up.

But still sleep eluded her as she began to recall what Lewis had said about Rebecca Cunningham's phone call and the possibility of the imminent return of herself and her husband. Once that happened this strange little interlude in her life would be over. She would move back to her studio flat, Lewis would presumably move back to his apartment, the children would settle down to life with their parents again and everything would return to normal.

But wasn't that exactly what she wanted? Hadn't she been reluctant at the beginning to even take this on? Surely now that it was soon to be over she should be thankful?

She'd grown very fond of the children in the short time she had been caring for them—of serious little Alistair, mischievous Francesca and the adorable little Jamie. She would miss them terribly, she already knew that.

But was it only the children she would miss? What of their uncle, what of Lewis? Would she miss him also? Would she miss the intimacy that had grown between them? She knew the answer to that almost without thinking about it. Knew without a shadow of doubt that she would miss him.

There would still be work, of course. She would see him there. She brightened at that and eventually it was with that thought uppermost in her mind that she drifted off to sleep.

Jo dreaded facing Marcus on Monday morning. It was one thing to walk out on him during a date, but something else altogether to face him across the operating table and carry on working as if nothing had happened.

She half hoped it would be another surgeon on duty that day, but a quick look at the rota confirmed her worst fears when she saw it was Mr Hughes which, of course, meant Marcus would be assisting him.

'Don't let him get to you,' said Pru in a low voice as the two of them scrubbed up.

'That's easier said than done.' Jo pulled a face.

'Look, not many girls get one over on Marcus,' said Pru. 'You have. You weren't the pushover he thought you were. Don't spoil it now by letting him think you were bothered by what happened. It'll do him good to be taken down a peg or two.'

As it happened, she needn't have worried because, far from hassling her in any way, Marcus completely ignored her, not even acknowledging her presence in the theatre.

The patient, Timothy Roberts, was a boy for circumcision, and while Lewis was anaesthetising him Mr Hughes explained the history.

'This little chap had a congenital abnormality which resulted in a very tight foreskin, producing pain and finally infection,' he said. Glancing round at the team, then looking at Lewis, he went on, 'Are we ready, Lewis?'

'Nearly,' Lewis replied. 'I just want to give a further shot of local anaesthetic.'

'That's good.' Mr Hughes watched as Lewis administered the injection, then he turned to Jo and said, 'Right, Nurse, if you could cleanse and prepare, please, we can proceed.'

He paused while Jo carried out the cleansing of the baby's genital area and covered him with the green theatre drapes, then he said, 'I gather you all went to this Seventies bash on Saturday night?'

There were murmurings and nods from the rest of the team. Jo was careful not to look at Marcus.

'So, was it any good?'

More murmurs and nods.

'A few fat heads the next day, I dare say,' Mr Hughes went on. 'I can well remember the days when I went in for that sort of thing. Not now, though—much prefer a weekend's sailing.'

'How did it go, Edward?' asked Lewis as he checked the baby's breathing.

'Capital, old boy, absolutely capital,' said Edward. 'You missed a treat, I can tell you. Perfect conditions.'

'Yes, I dare say,' said Lewis. 'Still, it couldn't be helped and no doubt there'll be another time.'

'Oh, no doubt, no doubt. Scalpel, please, Nurse. Now, a nice little cut right here—that's it. Diathermy, please. Always a lot of blood with this op... So, tell me, Lewis, how long is this domestic situation of yours going on for?'

'Hard to say really,' said Lewis. 'My brother-in-law is responding to treatment now and apparently showing signs of improvement, which is good. But he isn't out of the woods yet and for a time there things really did look bad for him.'

'Ghastly business, some of these tropical diseases,' said the surgeon. Turning to Marcus, he said, 'Look at this. That was the problem this little chap had. Now, Nurse, can we have a suture in here, please, to help control the bleeding before I continue?'

As Jo leaned forward to carry out the surgeon's command Marcus stepped back and looked up. Briefly, very briefly, her gaze met his. His dark eyes above his mask were blank, expressionless, dead almost, and hastily she looked away, only to find herself meeting Lewis's gaze and realising that he had witnessed the look that had passed between herself and the houseman. What he had made of it, however, was anyone's guess.

When the operation was over Jo completed the suturing and applied a final dressing.

'There.' Edward Hughes stepped back and looked down at the baby as Jo removed the green drapes. 'That should make the little chap more comfortable. Handsome little fellow, isn't he?'

The baby was fair and bore a striking resemblance to Jamie. As the thought struck Jo she looked up quickly and caught Lewis's eye again. In that instant she knew the same thought had occurred to him. It was a special moment, one of shared intimacy between them and them alone, and somehow it helped to lighten the atmosphere in the theatre which, to Jo at least, had become unbearably oppressive.

The next few days followed a similar pattern to those of the previous week, with Jo and Lewis taking the children to Sue's each morning before going on to their work in the surgical day unit. Every afternoon Jo continued to pick up the two older children from school and Jamie from the child-minder, before returning to Chilterns and setting about the many chores that had to be done.

Lewis always helped her during the evenings—with the children's bath and bedtime, with the cooking of their own supper and the organisation of all that needed to be done to ensure the smooth running of the household.

One night he was called out again to an emergency and this time he was gone for the best part of the night. While he was out Jamie awoke and Jo, who by now was becoming acclimatised, heard him and tried to settle him. This proved to be difficult and he woke three more times during the night, the consequence being that throughout the following day both Jo and Lewis seemed to function purely on autopilot and by the evening were both wandering about in a daze.

'I don't know how people cope with all this on a long-term basis.' Jo sighed as she sank down onto the sofa, after reading the children their bedtime stories.

'I suppose they just get used to it,' said Lewis with a yawn.

'Did you say that Rebecca runs her own business?'

'Yes, she designs and markets greetings cards.'

'I don't know how she finds the time or where she gets the energy from.'

'Would you like to see some of her work?' asked Lewis, as if the thought had only just occurred to him.

'I should love to,' said Jo.

'Come on, then, I'll take you up to her studio.'

'Will she mind?' asked Jo as she struggled to her feet and followed Lewis out of the sitting room.

'No, of course not. She'd be pleased that you're interested.'

The studio was on the top floor of the house in what had once been the attics. Huge skylights had been installed in the roof, together with a large desk, working units and a drawing board. The worktops were littered with a vast array of paints, pens, pencils, charcoal and all the other requirements of a busy design artist.

'Becky always seems to work in a glorious muddle,' said Lewis. 'She says she's suspicious of a tidy workroom.'

'I love her style,' said Jo, gazing around in fascination at the pictures that covered the walls and the drawing board. Most were of wildlife—birds, animals or flowers—but others were fantasy themes—fairies, dragons and witches. 'She seems to combine the traditional with a slight surrealism—the effect is stunning.'

'She's always been highly creative and very imaginative,' said Lewis. He spoke casually but his pride in his sister was only too obvious.

'Do you have a photograph of her?' asked Jo. Suddenly she was curious about this woman whose home she was staying in, whose children she was taking care of.

'I think there are some albums downstairs,' Lewis replied. 'I'll see if I can find them.'

'I'll make the hot chocolate,' said Jo as they left the studio and went quietly downstairs.

Ten minutes later Jo carried a tray with two steaming mugs of chocolate into the sitting room. Setting the tray down on a coffee-table, she went and sat beside Lewis who was sitting on the sofa with an open photograph album across his knees.

'That's her,' he said. 'That's Becky. It was taken a couple of years ago but it's typically her.'

A young woman with laughing eyes and dark, wind-blown hair smiled up at them out of a photo-

graph obviously taken in the back garden of
Mowbery House.

'You aren't at all alike,' said Jo slowly.

'Becky's the image of our mother.' Lewis turned
several pages of the album. 'Look, there she is. And
this one here with my father.'

'Who you obviously take after,' said Jo quietly,
staring down at a picture of a man in the uniform of
the Royal Air Force who gazed solemnly back at
them.

'Yes, I guess so,' said Lewis.

Jo was silent for a moment then, half turning to
him, she said, 'How old were you when they died?'

'I was seventeen. Becky was nearly fifteen.'

'That must have been terrible for you...what happened?' She would never have asked him questions
of this nature only a very short time ago, but now
things had changed. Until recently she would never
have believed she would be sitting on a sofa late at
night with Lewis Gregson, consultant anaesthetist at
St Theresa's, looking through his family albums.

'It was a traffic accident,' he said. 'They were on
holiday in the Lake district. A lorry went out of control on a sharp bend and hit their car. My mother was
killed instantly, my father died later in hospital.'

'What happened to you and Rebecca? Did you live
alone?'

'No, we lived with our grandparents. After I'd
qualified we did live together for a time while Becky

was at art school. After she married David I got myself an apartment, where I still live. Becky lives in
eternal hope that one day I will marry, settle down
and have a family.' He spoke lightly but Jo sensed
sudden tension in his voice.

'And you?' she said softly. 'Is that what you
want?'

He sighed. 'It was certainly what I wanted once
but since my engagement ended—I don't know. I
sometimes doubt it'll ever happen now.'

There was a bitterness in his tone now and Jo was
aware just how badly he had been hurt. Moving
away, she took one of the mugs from the table and
handed it to him. Then she picked up her own, curled
her hands around it and began sipping the chocolate.

After a time Lewis began to turn the pages of the
album again, pointing out photographs, reminiscing
and recalling happy events.

It was warm in the sitting room and comfortable
on the sofa, and as both Jo and Lewis relaxed the
weariness that had crept up on them both throughout
the day gradually overtook them.

When Jo opened her eyes it was to find Alistair
standing in front of her and tugging at her sleeve.
Lewis was sound asleep at her side and she realised
that her head had been resting on his shoulder and
the photograph album was still open on his lap.

'Alistair!' Jo stared at the little boy, then struggled

to get up. 'What is it? What's wrong? Is it Jamie? Is he crying?'

'No.' Alistair shook his head. 'It's not Jamie, it's Francesca—I think she's had a bad dream.'

At the moment Lewis awoke, also struggling to get his bearings. By this time Jo was on her feet. 'It's Francesca,' she muttered as she fought through the mists of sleep. 'She's had a nightmare. I'll go to her.'

She followed Alistair, trying desperately to cope with the effects of pins and needles in one leg and the waves of dizziness from getting up too quickly, while at the same time vaguely aware that Lewis was following them but more slowly as he, too, struggled to reorientate himself.

She found Francesca sitting bolt upright in her bed, her eyes staring and her breath coming in hiccuping sobs. Sitting on the side of the bed, Jo gathered the little girl into her arms and held her tight.

'It's all right,' she soothed, smoothing the damp curls back from her hot little forehead. 'It's all right. You're quite safe.'

'Mummy!' cried the little girl. 'Mummy!' At the same time she wound her arms around Jo's neck and clutched her as if she would never let her go.

Jo held her for some time, only too aware of the child's pounding heart. As the unknown terrors gradually subsided, she glanced at the open doorway where Lewis stood, watching, with Alistair. 'It's all right,' said Jo. 'She's all right.'

'I think it's time we got you back to bed, young man,' said Lewis, looking down at Alistair. 'You did a grand job, looking after Francesca. Come on, I'll come to your room with you.'

Eventually Francesca's grip on Jo lessened, her eyelids drooped and at last Jo knew she had slipped back to sleep. Gently she disentangled herself and laid the little girl down on her pillow. She covered her with her duvet and sat for a moment looking down at her, before leaning forward and dropping a gentle kiss on her cheek.

In the short time she had been with these children she had grown to care about them. She had grown so fond of them all that she was already beginning to wonder how she was going to cope when she had to say goodbye to them, knowing how much she would miss them in the weeks to come.

When at last she tiptoed from the room it was to find Lewis standing on the landing, waiting for her.

'Is she all right?' he whispered.

'Yes,' Jo replied, 'she's fine. She's asleep now.'

'Alistair's gone back to sleep as well,' said Lewis. 'And talking of sleep, I would say it's high time we got to bed.'

'What is the time?' asked Jo. 'I've got no idea at all.'

'It's half past two,' Lewis replied, ruefully glancing at his watch.

'In that case, I guess you're right,' Jo replied. 'Before we know where we are it'll be time to get up and to go to work.'

For a long moment they stared at each other in the dim light, then Lewis leaned forward and very gently touched her lips with his own in a kiss so light, so gentle, that afterwards Jo was to wonder if she might have imagined it.

For the first few days after the Seventies night Jo was blissfully unaware of the rumours that were circulating the day unit, but as the week went on she very gradually began to realise that she was on the receiving end of smiles and sniggers and that she was the object of meaningful glances between other members of staff.

She put up with it for a time, at first thinking she was imagining it and later, when she became convinced that she wasn't, by simply hoping it would go away. When, however, it showed no sign of abating and, if anything, got worse, she decided to tackle Pru about it.

'Don't know what you mean,' said Pru when Jo tracked her down in the staffroom, but she looked embarrassed and it was clear that she did know.

'Please,' said Jo, 'tell me, Pru. I know there's something going on but I don't know what it is and until I do know I can't do anything about it.'

'It's just gossip really.' Pru looked more uncomfortable than ever. 'I tried to put paid to it for you myself but you know what people are and how they relish getting their teeth into something.'

'I can't imagine what it is they've got their teeth into...' Jo looked bewildered, but when Pru wouldn't meet her gaze she narrowed her eyes and said, 'Does it have anything to do with me staying with Lewis?'

'Well...that's partly it,' said Pru uneasily.

'Only partly! What else is there, for heaven's sake? I haven't been here long enough to give them anything else to gossip about and I certainly haven't had the time to even go anywhere...except for...' She stopped and stared at Pru as a niggling realisation suddenly dawned on her. 'Does this have anything to do with Marcus?'

'I think that's where it started,' admitted Pru. 'But listen, Jo, the best thing to do is simply to ignore it.'

'I want to know what he's been saying,' said Jo quietly.

'No,' said Pru. 'No, Jo, you don't.'

'Yes, I do. I want to know now, Pru, and if you don't tell me I shall go and ask someone else.'

'Oh, very well.' Pru gave a deep sigh. 'Have it your own way. But don't say I didn't warn you. It was after the Seventies night...'

'I gathered that much,' said Jo grimly. 'So, what has he been saying?'

'Well, for a start he told Gary Kent that Gary had lost his bet—'

'What?' Jo stared at her in dismay.

'Told you you wouldn't like it. He said...' Pru paused. 'He said you were more than ready to fall into bed with him.'

Jo drew in her breath sharply. 'So how does he explain the fact that we have barely spoken to each other since?' she demanded.

'Ah, well, I said there was more, didn't I? He said that after that first time he found out you were living with Lewis Gregson, and that he wasn't prepared to associate with slags.... Sorry, Jo.' Pru helplessly spread her hands as Jo stared at her in disbelief. 'But that's it. I did my utmost to defend you. Whenever I've heard anyone talking about it, I've said it's absolute rubbish.'

'But are you saying that people are choosing to believe it?' Jo continued to stare at Pru in growing dismay.

'I'm not sure that people believe Marcus's boasting. After all, they all know him of old. No, the real problem lies with the fact that you're living in the same house as Lewis Gregson.'

'But I'm working for him, for heaven's sake!' Jo protested.

'You know that and I know that,' said Pru. 'But try telling those who are hell-bent on reading something into it, especially when Marcus has already fuelled the flames. Sorry, Jo, you simply can't help people making of it what they will.'

'What can I do?' asked Jo in desperation.

'Not a lot. Just lie low. It'll be a nine-day wonder then they'll start on someone else. Besides, didn't you say you'll be going back to your flat soon?'

Jo nodded. 'Yes, the children's mother will be home in a few days.'

'Well, there you are, then. There won't be any cause for gossip then. Anyway—' Pru brightened a bit '—wasn't it you who said you didn't care about what people think?'

'Yes, yes, I did,' said Jo slowly.

'So what are you worrying about? It'll go away—you'll see.'

It was true, Jo thought as the two of them left the staffroom and hurried back to the ward, she didn't usually care what people thought. So why was she bothered about this? She knew the answer to that. While she might not care what other people thought, she cared very much what Lewis might think. He might not think anything about the gossip about them living together, might even laugh about it because he would know there was nothing in those rumours, but the rumours about her having slept with Marcus Jacobs were another thing altogether. The last thing Jo wanted was that he might not only hear those rumours but, far worse, might actually believe them.

CHAPTER TEN

'DELLA. Della Latham?'

'Yes, that's me.' A tall, slim, young woman with shoulder-length, honey blonde hair flung down the glossy magazine she had been reading and rose to her feet.

'Would you come this way, please?' said Jo, leading the way down the short corridor to the ward. 'Now…' She paused at the foot of the first bed inside the door. 'If you'd like to get undressed and put on this theatre gown…' she indicated the white gown neatly folded on the bed '…then slip your dressing-gown on top. I'll be back in a few minutes to check your details. After that the doctor and the anaesthetist will be along to see you.' She glanced at the list in her hand. 'I understand you're having a cyst removed from your leg—is that correct?'

'Yes.' Della Latham nodded. As Jo would have moved away she said, 'Tell me, who exactly is the anaesthetist?'

'As far as I know it'll be Mr Gregson,' Jo replied.

'Lewis Gregson?'

'Yes, that's right.' Jo nodded. 'Do you know him?'

167

'Oh, yes.' The woman smiled. 'Lewis and I know each other from way back.'

Jo had no further time to speculate as to where or when this patient and Lewis may have known each other for at that moment Janet Luscombe bustled into view and Jo hastily took herself off to check the details of another patient.

She didn't recall the incident again until later when she had taken and checked Della Latham's particulars and Lewis himself had started his round. Because Jo was actually inside the cubicle she witnessed the moment when Lewis opened the curtains.

Della Latham was sitting on the bed but she half turned and looked up at the anaesthetist. 'Hello, Lewis,' she said softly.

He stopped and, knowing him as well as she now did, Jo could tell he was surprised, shocked even.

'Della!' he said. 'This is a surprise. I had no idea it was you.'

'I doubt you knew the name,' she said with a short laugh. 'After all, you never did meet Philip, did you?'

'No, I didn't.' Lewis shook his head. 'So, how is married life?' he added.

'I've forgotten. We were divorced two years ago.' She gave a shrug then, with a curious glance in his direction, she narrowed her eyes and said, 'And what about you? Married with a couple of kids by now, I dare say.'

'No, not at all.' He shook his head and then, apparently recovering, he slipped once more into professional mode and went on briskly, 'I understand you are to have a cyst removed from your leg. May I see it, please?'

'Of course.' Deftly Della Latham pulled up the white theatre gown to reveal the rather large lump on her left thigh. 'There it is. Unsightly, isn't it? I can't wait to be rid of it.' All the time she was speaking her eyes never left Lewis's face.

'Right. I see.' Lewis nodded. 'Well, Mr Hughes and I have discussed this and we've agreed that a local anaesthetic should be sufficient so there will be no need to put you to sleep.'

'I won't feel anything, will I?' Her eyes widened slightly.

'No, of course not,' Lewis replied. 'You can trust me.'

'Oh, I know that.' She laughed.

After they had discussed allergies and medication Jo left the cubicle with Lewis. 'Sounds like you two go back a long way,' she said lightly when they were well out of earshot.

'You're right.' He nodded. 'We do. We grew up in the same town. Went to the same school.'

'Really?' Jo was surprised to find she was experiencing a stab of something that could only be envy, or possibly jealousy, that this woman, whoever she was, seemed to know much more about Lewis

Gregson than she did. She had known him as a child, had attended the same school, had played childhood games with him and knew a side of him that was probably gone for ever. But Jo had no time to speculate any further as the busy ward routine took over and demanded her full attention.

Apart from escorting Della Latham to the anaesthetics room, Jo saw little more of her and when she eventually went off duty at lunchtime Della was back on the ward, resting quietly after her operation.

After collecting the children from school and Jamie from Sue Meadows, Jo took them all to the park where for an hour they fed the ducks on the pond, played ball and spent time on the adventure playground.

On their return to Chilterns they found that Lewis had returned from work and was waiting for them in the open doorway.

'I have some news for you,' he said. Jo threw him a quick glance as he took Jamie from her but was reassured to see he was smiling. 'Your mum phoned—they are being flown home tomorrow.'

The children began cheering and squealing and dancing around the forecourt while Jo stared at Lewis, surprised to find that on hearing this news her feelings were quite mixed. While she was naturally delighted that David Cunningham was obviously on the mend, and that the children were about to be reunited with their parents, the news of their return signified that her duties at Chilterns were almost at an end.

'It's amazing really,' Lewis went on as they went into the house. 'David has responded so well to the treatment that it appears it won't even be necessary for him to go to a hospital that specialises in tropical diseases—he's being transferred directly to St Theresa's.'

'That's marvellous,' said Jo.

'It'll certainly be easier for Becky,' agreed Lewis. 'What with the children and visiting and everything else.'

'Do you think she'll want us to stay on for a while when she first gets home?' asked Jo as she pushed open the kitchen door and dumped her bag onto the floor.

'I don't know. She may well need a bit of extra help for a day or two. But...' Lewis paused and looked at Jo over the top of Jamie's head. 'Would you be prepared to do that? You must be longing to get back to the peace and quiet of your own flat.'

'It's OK.' She gave a little shrug. 'I don't mind, really I don't.' She turned away and began unpacking her bag, the bits and pieces of shopping that she had picked up from the supermarket on the way home. If the truth be known she was dreading the quiet and solitude of her flat. Whereas once it had been all she had craved, now—after her taste of the warmth, love and laughter of family life—it was the last thing in the world she wanted.

And, of course, it would also mean being without Lewis and that was the thing she dreaded most, was dreading so much, in fact, that she was afraid to even try to analyse her feelings for fear of recognising the truth.

'Mummy's coming home,' Francesca whispered that night when Jo bent to kiss her goodnight. Lewis had been called back to the hospital and Jo had put the children to bed on her own.

'Yes, darling, I know. It'll be lovely for you to be all together again.'

'What about you?' The little girl's dark eyes grew anxious.

'What do you mean, what about me?' said Jo.

'You won't have to go, will you?'

'Well, yes, eventually I'll have to go.'

'But why?' wailed Francesca.

'Because I have a home of my own,' said Jo.

'But I don't want you to go. I want you to stay.' Francesca wound her arms around Jo's neck and held her tightly. 'And I want Uncle Lew to stay as well.'

'I'll come back to see you,' Jo promised. 'And I'm sure Uncle Lewis comes to see you all the time, doesn't he?'

'Yes.' Francesca gave a little hiccup. 'But it won't be the same as you being here. I'm going to ask Mummy if you can stay.'

There was more of the same from Alistair but in a slightly different vein. 'Do you think Dad will soon be better?' he asked anxiously, after Jo had read him his story.

'We hope so,' she replied cautiously. 'It certainly sounds as if he's much better than he was.'

'He won't be able to play football, will he?'

'I wouldn't have thought so. I guess he'll need to rest for quite some time.'

'That's what I thought,' said Alistair gloomily. Then, brightening a little, he said, 'Maybe Uncle Lew will still play football with me.'

'I'm sure he will.' Jo smiled. 'I'm sure he'll come over and see you a lot.'

'And what about you, Jo? Will you come and see us as well?' asked Alistair. He said it so earnestly it brought a lump to Jo's throat.

'Yes,' she said. 'Of course I will.'

'That's all right, then,' said Alistair, and with a contented little sigh he settled down to sleep.

Jo was in little doubt of just how important she had become in the lives of these children and it gave her a warm glow somewhere deep inside whenever she thought about it. What was less clear was whether or not she was in any way important to their uncle or whether, when their duties ended on the return of the children's parents, he would simply forget the times they had shared and she would become just another colleague once more.

These uncertainties persisted throughout the remainder of that evening as she finished the chores and still Lewis failed to return from the hospital. By the time she at last retired to bed she found herself forced to face the heady possibility that she might be falling in love with him. Until that moment she had refused to even contemplate such a thing, but now, forced to face the inevitable change that would shortly take place, she knew she could deny it no longer.

Whether or not there was the remotest chance he might feel the same way was another matter altogether, something which would have to be faced in the future, but for the time being Jo only knew the overwhelming certainty of her own feelings.

'Mummy! Mummy!' An ecstatic Francesca hurled herself into the arms of the tall, dark-haired young woman who alighted from the taxi at the front entrance of Chilterns. Alistair held back, but only for a moment. As the woman crouched down and opened her arms even wider to include him as well, he, too, rushed forward and buried his face against her shoulder.

'Oh, my darlings. It's so good to see you again.' Rebecca Cunningham was laughing and crying at the same time. 'And Jamie…where's Jamie?'

'There he is.' Francesca extricated herself from her mother's embrace and turned towards Jo, who was standing quietly in the doorway with Jamie in her arms as she watched the touching reunion.

Slowly Rebecca straightened up once more, her gaze meeting Jo's as she moved forward. 'You must be Jo,' she said, her ready smile widening.

'Yes, that's right.' Jo smiled back then held out the baby.

Tears and smiles mingled afresh as Rebecca was reunited with Jamie. As she cuddled him they all moved into the house, the children on either side of her, holding onto her arms and tugging at her sleeves.

As the taxi drew away Lewis, having paid the driver, turned and looked at Jo. 'Shall we go in?' he said softly.

She nodded, doubting at that moment whether she could trust her voice, and together they followed the little group into the house.

'How did David stand up to the flight?' asked Lewis later, after Rebecca had unpacked and joined them in the kitchen where Jo had brewed a pot of tea and Francesca had arranged flapjacks on a plate.

'Better than I'd feared,' said Rebecca as she sank down wearily onto a chair and kicked off her shoes. 'He was tired, of course—exhausted really—but that was only to be expected. But he's now safely installed in the medical ward at St Theresa's.'

'I'll go in and see him later,' said Lewis. 'How much longer will he be on the treatment? Has anyone said?'

'Another five days,' said Rebecca. 'After that, provided all goes well, they say he'll be able to come home to convalesce.'

'It's not going to be too easy for you for the next few days,' said Lewis, taking the mug of tea Jo passed to him across the table.

'I haven't thought that far ahead,' said Rebecca with a sigh. 'My main priority was getting him back to this country.'

'We were wondering,' Lewis went on, 'Jo and I, that is, if you'd like us to stay on to help out just until David comes home.'

'Oh, yes!' cried Francesca.

'Well, that's very kind of you.' Rebecca looked from one to the other. 'But, really, I can't impose on you both any longer—you've done more than enough as it is.'

'Nonsense,' said Lewis briskly. 'We don't mind and, besides, how do you think you'll manage with visiting and everything? Anyway, it won't be for long. I can move into the boxroom for a few nights and you can have your bedroom back, Becky.'

'It looks like it's settled, then,' said Rebecca.

'Yes!' Alistair punched the air and Francesca began hopping up and down from one foot to the other.

'I'm going to be a bluebell, Mummy,' she said excitedly. 'Aren't I, Jo?'

'Yes, that's right.' Jo nodded and smiled at the little girl.

'I can see I have lots to catch up on,' said Rebecca, sipping her tea.

'Yes,' agreed Alistair solemnly. 'Lots. For a start I'm in the school football team. You didn't know that, did you?'

'It really was very good of you, putting your life on hold to help my family out,' said Rebecca.

It was much later. Lewis and Rebecca had returned from the hospital where they had been to visit David, the children were in bed and Lewis was upstairs, telling them their bedtime stories while Jo prepared spaghetti Bolognese for supper.

'It helped me, actually, as well,' said Jo.

'Really?' Rebecca looked up quickly.

'Yes, I only have a part-time job at the moment, you see—I was getting a bit desperate for more hours.'

'You must have been desperate to take on my lot,' said Rebecca with a laugh.

'They're lovely children,' said Jo.

'They can also be a handful as I know only too well.'

They were silent for a moment, then Jo became aware that Rebecca was watching her. 'Lewis tells me you work together,' she said at last.

Jo nodded. 'Sort of,' she said, 'although there's a bit of difference between my job and that of an anaesthetist.'

'I disagree,' said Rebecca. 'As far as I'm concerned, one depends on the other.'

'Well, I guess that's one way of looking at it.' Jo paused. 'I shall have to be looking for something else, though—I can't survive on the hours I'm doing.'

'Maybe something will come up in another department,' said Rebecca sympathetically.

'Maybe, yes,' agreed Jo. That, she knew, on the one hand would be the ideal solution, but it would also mean she would no longer be working with Lewis and somehow that was something she didn't even want to contemplate. Not living together in the same house after this week, that would be quite bad enough, without not seeing each other on the day unit as well.

'So, did you and Lewis know each other, apart from working together?' asked Rebecca after a moment.

'No,' Jo replied, recognising the inevitable curiosity of a sister behind Rebecca's words, even though she spoke casually. 'No, we'd never met before. I've only recently come to Queensbury to work.'

'Lewis must have thought very highly of you to ask you to come here and look after the children,' said Rebecca thoughtfully.

'I think it may have been more desperation than anything else,' replied Jo with a laugh. 'In fact, you

could say it was a case of two desperate people together.'

'Don't underestimate yourself—he thinks the
world of the children and he'd never entrust them to
just anyone. He'd have to be sure that person was
every bit as capable as he is.'

'I must admit he really is very good with them,'
agreed Jo.

'He's a natural,' said Rebecca, taking a bottle of
wine from the rack and studying the label. 'He
should be married with kids of his own, of course,
and if things had worked out right…that's exactly
what would have happened.'

'He said he was engaged once…' said Jo slowly.
She wasn't sure she even wanted to pursue this topic
of conversation but she was almost consumed by a
morbid sort of curiosity about the woman Lewis was
to have married.

'Unfortunately,' Rebecca went on, and Jo couldn't
help but notice that her tonc had changed, become
tighter almost contemptuous, 'to the wrong person. I
live in hopes that he'll meet someone else, but…'
She shook her head doubtfully.

'You don't think he will?' Jo had been about to
strain the spaghetti but she paused and glanced at
Rebecca.

'It hit him very badly when his fiancée betrayed
him. There was a point when I didn't think he was
ever going to get over it. They'd known each other

since they were children, you see, and he loved her so very much—'

Rebecca broke off suddenly as they heard a sound in the hall. 'He's coming,' she said quickly. 'Let's change the subject. I'd hate him to think we'd been discussing him.'

'Yes, of course.' Jo turned back to the sink, and as Lewis came through the door she said, 'Your work must be fascinating, Rebecca. Lewis showed me your designs. I hope you don't mind.'

'Not at all.'

'I love your style...'

The moment passed easily as they drifted into another conversation, but Jo was left with yet another insight into the man she now knew without a shadow of doubt she was in love with.

The following day Jo was in Theatre again, and was nearing the end of the morning's list when Lewis caught her eye. 'I'm going up to see David,' he said. 'I wondered if you would like to come with me.'

'I should like to, yes, that is if you don't think it will be too tiring for him,' Jo replied.

'We needn't stay for too long,' said Lewis. 'I just thought it would be nice for David to meet you.'

'You two really are getting pally, aren't you?' said Pru as Lewis moved away.

'What do you mean?' Jo was aware that her cheeks had flushed.

'Well, what was all that about? I couldn't help

overhearing. He wanted you to visit someone with him.'

'Yes, his brother-in-law,' Jo replied.

'You mean he's home?' Pru's eyes widened. She'd been on leave for a couple of days and Jo hadn't had the chance to tell her of the recent developments in the Cunningham household.

'Yes, they were flown home yesterday. He's upstairs on Medical.'

'Really?' Pru looked amazed. 'It sounded like he was at death's door only a few days ago.'

'Oh, he was. I don't doubt that,' said Jo quickly. 'But the treatment that was flown out by his company has apparently worked miracles.'

'So, presumably, his wife is now back at the helm?' A speculative gleam had come into Pru's eyes.

'Well, yes, sort of…'

'So you'll be going home?'

'Eventually.'

'Aren't you going straight away?'

'Not exactly.' Jo hesitated. 'Lewis decided it might be a good idea if we were to stay on for a few days to help out.'

'Oh, yes?' The gleam in Pru's eyes grew even more speculative.

'Well, it makes sense,' said Jo, rushing to defend the decision. 'After all, Rebecca has to visit her husband while he's in hospital, and there are the children...'

'I dare say there are many women in that position who would like the sort of back-up that you and the hunky Lewis are providing,' said Pru, 'but they just have to soldier on. It's OK.' She laughed when she caught sight of Jo's troubled expression. 'It's very commendable of you both, I'm sure. It just means, of course, that it'll prolong the current situation for a while longer, but I'm sure no one will make anything of that.' With a wink she took herself off to the sluice, leaving Jo feeling decidedly uneasy.

The man in the hospital bed, propped up against a mountain of pillows, looked grey and much older than his thirty-eight years. His hair was lank and sparse and his gaunt face drawn from the amount of weight he had lost, but the gaze he turned on Jo was bright and full of interest as she stood beside the bed with Lewis.

'So you're the lady I have to thank for holding my family together in their time of need,' he said, a weary smile tugging at the side of his mouth.

'Hardly that,' Jo protested. 'Lewis really is the one who should take the credit. He was coping long before I came onto the scene.'

'Ah,' said Lewis solemnly. 'But you were the one who was there to bail me out when the going really got tough.'

'Well, whoever it was, I am truly grateful,' said David. 'I gather it was touch and go there for me for a time and I know it must have been a tremendous comfort to Rebecca, knowing the children were well looked after.'

'Treatment is going well, I gather,' said Lewis, moving round the bed to pick up David's chart and study it.

'If you can call a cross between sandblasting and a dose of mild explosives going well then, yes, I suppose it is,' said David. 'God only knows what that bug was that got hold of me, but whatever it was I would say it was only marginally worse than the drug they're using to flush it out.'

'You're going to have to take things easy for a time,' said Lewis. 'No burning the candle at both ends like you usually do.'

'I know.' David sighed.

'Maybe it will have its compensations,' said Jo.

'I must admit I haven't thought of too many,' David replied drily.

'Well, at least you'll get to see more of your family and I'm sure they won't be complaining about that.'

'Are you saying you don't think I spend enough time with my family?' David turned to look at her but the effort almost proved too much for him and, exhausted, he leaned back against the pillows again and closed his eyes.

Jo flushed. 'I'm sorry,' she said. 'I wasn't meaning to criticise but I just think it'll be nice for you to be able to see Alistair play for his school and to go to Francesca's ballet performance.'

David opened his eyes again and looked at her. 'Point taken,' he said.

'You actually managed to say what the rest of us have been thinking for a very long time,' said Lewis a few minutes later as he and Jo made their way downstairs, leaving David to rest. 'David is away far too much. He sees next to nothing of Rebecca or his children. In fact, it was reaching the stage where they were beginning to relate to me more than to their father.'

'Well, maybe it's taken this to make him see it and, hopefully, change his lifestyle a bit,' said Jo. 'If he doesn't, I'm sure in years to come he'll live to regret it. After all, children grow up so fast and those precious moments can never be repeated.'

'You can say that again,' said Lewis. 'Let's hope that in future David sees that his wife and children are the most important things in his life.'

As Lewis took himself off to his consulting room Jo found herself wondering if he, too, might realise the same thing and come to the conclusion that it was time he moved on after his disastrous engagement and once again find someone to share his own life.

CHAPTER ELEVEN

JO AND Lewis remained with the Cunninghams for a
further week. Rebecca visited David each afternoon
while Jo continued to pick the children up from their
schools and Jamie from the child-minder, just as she
had done while Rebecca was away. In the evenings
Lewis would help with baths and bedtime then he
and Jo would prepare supper while Rebecca returned
to the hospital. Later the three of them would eat
together.

With the easing of pressure in the household it was
a pleasant time full of chat and laughter, and Jo
found the thought of the return to normality even
more of a dread with the passing of each day. Since
Rebecca's return there had been very little opportunity of being alone with Lewis, and even those
strange middle-of-the-night encounters became a
thing of the past as Rebecca resumed responsibility
for Jamie's nocturnal requirements.

Jo was still uncertain of Lewis's feelings towards
her as the memory of their special shared moments
faded. He made no further attempt to seek her out,
either at work or at home, and as the week passed
her despair grew.

Maybe he had heard the rumours that had circulated about her and, even worse, had believed them.

Marcus continued to be cool and distant, much to Jo's relief. She really didn't feel she could cope with any more of his nonsense.

And then one evening the inevitable happened and Rebecca announced that David was to be discharged from hospital in a couple of days' time.

'That's great,' said Lewis. 'He won't look back now, Becky, you'll see.'

'I do hope you're right.' Rebecca sighed. 'It'll certainly be lovely to have him home again. And...' she turned to Lewis and Jo who were sitting opposite her at the kitchen table '...you two will be able to have your lives back again. I really don't know what we'd have done without you.'

'We've got an idea!' At the sudden announcement they all turned to the doorway where Alistair and Francesca stood. Both children looked triumphant, almost bursting with suppressed excitement, Alistair with his face red and shining and Francesca's bright dark eyes peeping mischievously through the black tangle of her hair.

'So what's this idea?' asked Rebecca with a laugh.

'We think,' said Alistair solemnly, 'that Uncle Lew and Jo should get married.'

'Get married...' echoed Francesca.

'Oh, really?' said Rebecca. She answered seriously

but a smile hovered around her mouth. 'And why do you think that?'

'Well,' said Alistair in the same solemn voice, 'if they did, that would make Jo our auntie, wouldn't it?'

'That's right,' Rebecca agreed, 'it would.'

'I'd like that,' said Francesca, 'because she would come and see us lots and lots of times.'

'I'll do that anyway,' said Jo quickly. 'I told you I would.'

'You might forget,' said Alistair.

'But if you were our auntie you would come every time Uncle Lew comes,' said Francesca, 'and he comes lots of times…and…and we go and see him…and if you were married to him, you'd live with him and you'd always be there in his house.'

'So that's why we think it would be a good idea,' concluded Alistair.

'I pretended they were our mummy and daddy when you were away, didn't I, Jo?' said Francesca.

'Yes, darling, you did,' said Jo. Suddenly she found she couldn't look at either Lewis or at Rebecca.

'Well?' said Alistair. 'What do you think?'

It was Rebecca, mercifully, who took over. 'It's not that simple, you know,' she said gently.

'Why?' demanded Francesca.

'Well, before two people get married they have to be in love,' explained Rebecca patiently.

'Oh, that,' said Alistair scornfully. 'Well, that's no problem.'

'Oh?' Rebecca raised her eyebrows. 'Why's that?'

'Uncle Lew does love Jo,' said Francesca.

'Well, I'm sure he likes Jo,' said Rebecca. 'We all do.'

'He loves her,' said Francesca firmly.

'I guess he must do,' said Alistair gloomily, 'to actually want to kiss her. I guess you really would have to love anyone to want to kiss them…and to cuddle them, on the sofa, in the middle of the night.'

'I hadn't realised,' said Rebecca later when she and Jo were alone in the kitchen.

'Realised what?' said Jo.

'That there was anything between you and Lewis. But, I must say, I'm delighted—'

'There isn't,' Jo interrupted, her voice flat, lifeless.

'Isn't? But the children? I know they get carried away sometimes, but they seemed so sure…'

'Wishful thinking, that's all,' said Jo firmly as she began stacking the dishwasher.

'Well, I did wonder about that, of course. I'm sure there's nothing they'd like better than to see you two together. But they must have thought…there must have been some indication for them to believe…'

'Like the kiss, you mean?' said Jo with a forced laugh.

'Well, yes, there is that, I suppose…'

'It was perfectly innocent. It happened when I agreed to take on the job of helping Lewis here. He was so pleased he gave me a kiss. It was simply a spontaneous gesture, that's all.'

'Of course…'

'Unfortunately Alistair happened to come into the room at that precise moment and he put a completely different interpretation on it—as children will.'

'Absolutely,' said Rebecca. There was a long pause. 'And the sofa incident?' she asked innocently. 'What was that all about?'

'It was one evening when we were both absolutely shattered. Lewis had been called out the previous night and I had been up with Jamie. Anyway, we both sat there…on the sofa…'

'Watching the telly?' asked Rebecca in the same innocent tones.

'Er, no. No, I don't think we were watching the telly. If I remember rightly…' Jo hesitated, anticipating how this would sound. 'Lewis was showing me some family photographs in one of your albums…'

'Really?' Rebecca's eyes, so like her daughter's, widened into dark pools.

'Rebecca, it really wasn't like it sounds,' Jo protested.

'I'm sure it wasn't,' said Rebecca, but Jo knew from the wicked look of suppressed merriment in her eyes that there was no way Rebecca was going to believe that.

And when, later, Francesca mercilessly went on to relay the episode of the breakfast tray, complete with bluebell, Jo gave up all further attempts.

'I, actually, go along with the children,' Rebecca told her on the night before she was due to return to her flat. 'I can't think of anything I would like better than to see you and Lewis get together. Like I told you, I despaired when Della ditched him. Never thought he'd get over it. Oh, I know he's quiet, reserved even, but when you really get to know him—'

'What did you say her name was?' Jo interrupted.

'Who?' Rebecca had been folding a pile of laundry—sheets and towels—but she paused and looked blankly at Jo.

'Lewis's fiancée—the one who left him?'

'Della, Della Masters.'

'Not Della Latham?' asked Jo slowly.

'No…' Rebecca frowned, shaking her head. 'Although, wait a minute,' she said a moment later, looking up, 'I think that may have been her married name. She had an affair with Lewis's best friend, John Richards. That's what broke up the engagement—when Lewis found out. The affair didn't last long, however, and soon afterwards we heard she'd got married. I think her husband's name was Philip something or other—it could well have been Latham. He had some computer business in Basingstoke.

'But—' Rebecca stared curiously at Jo '—why do you ask? Do you know her?'

'Not really,' Jo shook her head. 'I think I just came across the name somewhere, that's all.' She was deliberately evasive; she could never breach hospital confidentiality.

Della Latham had said that she and Lewis went back a long way but not for one moment had Jo suspected that she had been the person he had at one time hoped to marry.

Her suspicions were compounded even further a moment later when Rebecca went on, 'She's been in contact again with Lew, actually.'

Jo swallowed. 'Really?' she said.

'Yes. She phoned him here and apparently asked him to meet her somewhere for a drink and a chat.'

'And did he go?' asked Jo.

'Yes, I think so.' Rebecca paused reflectively. 'He was rather evasive about the whole thing. I only hope she doesn't cause any more trouble.'

'Do you think that's likely?'

'Oh, she's quite capable of causing havoc, believe me. Don't forget, I know her of old,' said Rebecca grimly. 'I also know the effect she had on Lew. I only hope he learnt his lesson where she was concerned and that he's got over her sufficiently since for her not to be a problem any longer.'

Maybe, Jo told herself later when she was alone in her room, this meeting with his ex-fiancée could in some way explain why Lewis had seemed so quiet in the last few days.

And maybe it could be the reason why he had made no further attempt to pursue any relationship with her.

Perhaps it had affected him badly, seeing Della again after all this time. After all, as Rebecca had said, he had been devastated when he had caught Della having an affair with his best friend. Maybe he never got over it.

And just maybe, Jo told herself miserably, he was still in love with her. Perhaps his apparent coolness and lack of response towards herself had nothing whatsoever to do with any rumours he may or may not have heard about her and Marcus Jacobs.

Maybe it was quite simply that he didn't want Jo reading anything into their relationship because it would never be anything other than one of employer and employee, and those moments of shared intimacy had been simply circumstantial and enforced—nothing more, nothing less.

And maybe the fact that Della had once betrayed him so badly was neither here nor there because now she was once again a free agent, having divorced her husband, and Lewis, too, was free to resume the relationship which had ended so abruptly all those years ago, leaving him so devastated.

Jo slept badly that night, her dreams haunted by images of Lewis with Della Latham and then of being pursued by some faceless demon who, when he finally caught her, turned out to be Marcus Jacobs.

When she awoke it was with a headache and she felt tired, unrefreshed and irritable, feelings which intensified even further when she remembered that this was the day she was to return to her flat.

'I don't want you to go, Jo,' wailed Francesca as Lewis carried bags from the house and stowed some in the boot of Jo's car and others in his own sports car. 'Nor Uncle Lew.'

'They'll be back to see you soon,' said Rebecca as she tried frantically to secure Jamie in his car seat, while at the same time trying to ensure that the other two children had everything they needed for the day ahead. 'And, just think, when you come home this afternoon, Daddy will be here!'

This seemed to console them a little but when Rebecca finally drove away in the Range Rover it was two very woebegone little faces that peered out of the back window.

'Popularity carries quite a responsibility,' observed Lewis quietly as he opened Jo's car door for her.

Because of the lump in her throat Jo found she was incapable of an answer. Neither could she bring herself to meet his gaze. Instead, all she could do was stand miserably as Lewis covered her hand briefly with his as she gripped the open edge of the car door.

'Thanks,' he said quietly. 'Thanks again for coming to my rescue.'

'Thanks for asking me.' Her voice was low, husky, not like her voice at all, and as they stood there together on the drive, suddenly she became so aware of him, his closeness, his very presence, that she longed for him to take her into his arms and for his lips to touch hers just as he had done before.

But it was not to be, and almost before it had begun the moment was over and Lewis drew away from her.

'I'll see you at the hospital,' he said, and his voice also sounded unusual, shaky almost, as if this parting affected him also, which, Jo told herself as they drove away, was probably quite ridiculous because, no doubt, Lewis couldn't wait to get his life back.

As it turned out, Jo hardly saw him at all that morning and before she knew it her shift was over and she was heading for her flat.

'I bet you can't wait,' Pru had said to her when she knew Jo was to return home that day. 'Just think, no more nappies, no more children's chatter and no more sleepless nights.'

And no more fun and laughter, Jo added silently, no more stories and cuddles and no more Lewis. No more shared meals or confidences, no more intimacies in the small hours of the night...the list seemed endless.

All there was now was an empty, cheerless flat, and by the end of that first evening Jo thought the silence would surely drive her mad.

'Have you heard the latest?' hissed Pru as she sidled in beside Jo in the scrub room.

'No. What now?' Jo's reply was only half-hearted. She really wasn't bothered what the latest gossip was or who had done what to whom.

Three days had passed since she'd left the Cunningham household and each day had been more miserable than the last. She'd hardly seen Lewis, and when she had he'd been friendly but polite and that was all.

By this time Jo had convinced herself that he must be seeing Della Latham again, even to the point where he had picked up their relationship where they had left it before.

'I thought this particular item might be of special interest to you,' said Pru as she plunged her hands into a bowl of water.

A niggle of suspicion suddenly touched Jo. What had Pru heard? Could this be it, precisely what she had been dreading? Had some shattering announcement already been made? Was she the last to know? Wildly she threw a sidelong glance at Pru.

'If this is about Lewis, I'm not sure that I want—'

'Lewis?' Pru looked blank. 'What are you talking about?'

'This gossip.'

'Of course not. The only gossip I've ever heard about Lewis was the fact that he was living with you!' Pru gave a peal of laughter. Then, throwing a quick glance over her shoulder to make sure they weren't being overheard, she said, 'No, this is about Marcus Jacobs.'

'Oh?' The stab of relief Jo felt was painful. 'What's he done now?'

'Bitten off more than he can chew, by the sounds of it. Apparently, and this is only what I've heard, he's been chatting up one of the new young secretaries, coming on really strong—you know what I mean.'

'Only too well,' said Jo tightly.

'Well, unbeknown to Marcus, this girl only turns out to be the niece of Edward Hughes. That was all kept pretty hush-hush because it seems old Teddy got her the job here. Anyway, when Marcus dropped her, because she wouldn't fall in with his demands, she was so angry that she reported him to her uncle. It seems she'd found out all about the wagers that go on. Anyway, I can't imagine old Teddy being too thrilled by Marcus's behaviour. He is his boss, after all…' She trailed off abruptly as the theatre sister came into the scrub room.

'Are you girls going to take all day in here?' she demanded waspishly.

'No, Sister,' said Pru. 'We're just coming.'

The first operation on the morning's list was a ligation of perforating veins and the patient was a middle-aged woman who also suffered with chronic bronchitis and who was very overweight. It was quite obvious from the start that Lewis was concerned about her breathing.

When Edward Hughes came into Theatre Jo found herself looking for Marcus. Somehow a chastened, subdued Marcus, stripped of his arrogance—although difficult to imagine—was a nevertheless intriguing prospect.

To her surprise, however, the surgeon was accompanied by another houseman that morning, a much younger man whom Jo had never met before.

'This is Andrew Biggs,' said Edward Hughes curtly. 'He will be assisting me today and for the foreseeable future.'

Jo looked up, startled, and very briefly her gaze met that of Lewis.

'Oh, boy,' whispered Pru in her ear. 'Looks like Casanova's got the boot. Maybe there's some justice in this world after all.'

The operation commenced with Mr Hughes explaining that the patient had suffered from oedema in her feet and ankles, followed by eczema and ulceration, finally resulting in grossly dilated veins which had subsequently perforated.

'Ideally I would have liked her to lose some weight before surgery,' the surgeon observed as he made his first incision in the patient's groin and Jo stepped forward with the diathermy machine to control the bleeding. 'When she found that impossible to achieve I decided we needed to proceed anyway. Everything all right with you, Lewis?'

'Yes, you can carry on, Edward,' Lewis replied. 'Like you say, a weightloss would have helped with her breathing, but she's doing all right at the moment.'

The operation commenced and that morning it seemed there was no room in the theatre for personal interactions. All gossip and innuendo was put aside as each of the team members' separate skills was brought into play. Then quite suddenly, when everything appeared to be progressing well, the alarm went off on the heart monitor and everyone stopped and looked up.

'Stop the operation, please,' said Lewis firmly.

Edward Hughes stepped back and Jo threw Lewis an anxious glance as he took control in the theatre.

'The patient's pulse and blood pressure have dropped,' said Lewis. He adjusted her airway and increased the oxygen, indicating to the ODA to bring him the appropriate drugs needed to increase her pulse. Then, with a quick glance at Jo, he said, 'Nurse, could you please control the bleeding?'

Jo stepped forward again and proceeded first to swab the wound then to apply diathermy again while

Lewis attached the stimulant drug to the intravenous cannula in the patient's hand.

After the drug had taken effect Lewis indicated for the operation to recommence and the team swung into action again.

There wasn't any light-hearted chat from Edward Hughes that day, either about sailing or anything else, and as the morning wore on and one patient followed another the atmosphere in the theatre seemed to grow more and more oppressive.

In the end Jo couldn't wait to escape. Being close to Lewis, yet at the same time so far, it was like some sort of torture, and by the time her shift was over she knew she wasn't sure quite how much longer she could bear it.

She was just leaving the nurses' station, after changing into her outdoor clothes, when Julian Browne, the charge nurse, came out of his office. 'Jo,' he said, 'have you got a minute?'

'Yes, of course.' She followed him, wondering what he wanted.

'I understand your little bit of moonlighting has come to an end?' Julian said as he closed the door behind her and indicated for her to sit down.

'My little bit of...?' She stared at him. 'Oh, that!' She laughed as she realised to what he was referring. 'Yes, unfortunately, it has.'

'You say unfortunately. Did you enjoy it?'

'Yes, actually, I did,' she said. 'But more to the point the extra money helped to pay a few bills.'

'Yes, quite. I can imagine.' Julian nodded. 'Actually, that was what I wanted to see you about.'

'Have you got more hours for me?' Eagerly Jo looked up.

'Yes, maybe.' Julian hesitated. 'Trouble is, it isn't on this unit.'

'Oh?' said Jo quickly.

'How would you feel about working on Paediatrics?'

'Well…' For a moment she didn't know what to say. Only a few days ago the last thing she would have wanted was a transfer to another department. Not to be working alongside Lewis, that would have been unthinkable. But now? Now maybe it was the answer. Especially if, as she suspected, he was seeing Della Latham again. That would be more than she could bear, seeing him every day, being so close to him and all the time knowing…imagining what was happening.

'I'll tell you what it is first,' said Julian, mistaking her hesitation. 'A full-time post has come up on Paediatrics for a senior staff nurse.'

'But that's a grade higher than me,' said Jo.

'I know that,' said Julian, 'but I'm prepared to give you a reference and so is Sister Taylor. We are both confident that you can do the job. Neither of us wants to lose you from here, of course, but we both know you need more hours and there's no sign of a full-time post coming up here for some considerable time. And, from what I hear, you like working with children.'

'Oh, yes, I do,' said Jo. 'Very much,' she added as a picture of Alistair, Francesca and Jamie came unbidden into her mind.

'In that case...' Julian stood up '...I suggest you get yourself an application form right away.'

'I will, Julian, and thank you,' said Jo. At the door she paused and looked back. 'One question,' she said.

'Yes?' Julian looked up.

'I understand Marcus Jacobs has been transferred. Can you tell me where?'

'Well, I'm afraid it isn't to Paediatrics,' Julian replied, misunderstanding the reason for her question.

'If it was, I wouldn't even be filling in the application form,' said Jo crisply.

It was quite late when the doorbell rang that evening. Jo had long since eaten her solitary meal and had spent the time since filling in the application form for her new job and watching a travel documentary on television. For one moment she was tempted not to answer the door, thinking it was probably only someone canvassing for something, but when a second ring came in rapid succession to the first and with a note of urgency about it, with a sigh she crossed the large room and opened the door the few inches the safety chain afforded.

Lewis stood on the step. 'It's OK, Jo,' he said. 'It's only me.'

In amazement and with her heart thudding uncomfortably Jo released the chain and flung back the door.

'Lewis,' she said faintly as he strode past her into the room. 'This is a surprise.'

It was the first time he had been in her flat and he prowled around for a moment, his gaze sweeping over her possessions—the heavy bleached calico spread on the bed-settee, the bright prints of Italian street scenes that adorned the walls, her plants and the flowers in the window-box beyond the open window where soft muslin curtains stirred softly in the evening breeze.

'This is nice,' he said, and she knew he meant it— wasn't just saying it for something to say. 'You've made this really nice.'

'Thank you,' she said, then waited, knowing he hadn't come just to see her flat.

'I'm sorry,' he said at last, 'to come like this, unannounced, but there's something I want to talk to you about.'

She stared at him and her heart sank. This was it. He had come to tell her that he was seeing Della again. That they had resumed their relationship. That he was going to marry her.

From the television behind her there came the familiar tune to a commercial for breakfast cereal. Ordinary, everyday sounds as life carried on as always. Did no one know or care that her world was about to end?

'You see, I know how you feel about him, but I can't stand it any longer. I only heard about it today and I guessed how you must be feeling so I had to come just to make sure you're all right.'

She frowned. Why didn't he just get on with it, for goodness' sake, tell her what he had come to say and get it over with? Then he could go and leave her to deal with her misery alone.

'I don't listen to gossip, you see,' he went on, 'so when something happens that everyone else seems to have been expecting to happen, I'm usually totally amazed. Like I was today when Edward Hughes told me what had been going on.'

Jo stared at him. 'I don't understand,' she said. 'What's this got to do with Edward Hughes?'

'Well, he's virtually sacked him, hasn't he? Had him moved to another department. I guess that in itself was bad enough for you, but this business with Edward's niece, well, that was something else. I really am sorry, Jo.'

'Lewis…' Jo took a deep breath. 'I'm sorry too, but I really don't have a clue what you're talking about.'

It was his turn to stare at her in bewilderment. 'I'm

talking about you,' he said. 'You and Marcus Jacobs.'

'Marcus Jacobs?' she echoed. 'I thought you'd come here to tell me about you. You and Della Latham.'

CHAPTER TWELVE

'Now, I'm afraid you've lost me,' said Lewis blankly. 'What's Della got to do with anything?'

Jo continued to stare at him, then her brain stopped idling and seemed to slip into gear. How could she tell him that she was devastated at the thought that he might be seeing Della again? What right had she to question anything he might do? On the other hand, and what at that moment seemed as if it might be even more intriguing, was this question of Marcus Jacobs and why Lewis felt he'd had to come to see her.

'I think,' she said, 'we'd better take this whole thing slowly, one step at a time. For a start let's go and sit down.'

'OK.' He nodded but he still looked bemused. Jo perched nervously on one end of the sofa while Lewis sat in the opposite corner. He looked casual in an expensive-looking pair of loafers, a wine-coloured rugby shirt and heavy cotton jeans. 'So, where shall we start?' he asked, tilting his head questioningly.

Jo felt her throat constrict with emotion. She loved him so much—how could she even contemplate the thought of the rest of her life without him?

She took a deep breath. 'You first,' she managed to say at last. 'You tell me why you're here and what it has to do with Marcus Jacobs.'

'Well…' Lewis considered. 'It was all that business about him and old Edward's niece—quite squalid stuff from what I can make out—and then him being reprimanded and moved to another department.'

'Yes,' said Jo. 'I knew all about that.' She paused, waiting for him to continue.

'I could only imagine how you must be feeling.' The glance he threw in her direction was almost sad. 'It must be tough enough, him going to another department—and the latest on that is that he may even be going to another hospital—but for you the reason for his departure must be pretty devastating. I'm sorry, Jo, I really am.' Lewis spread his hands, the gesture wholly sympathetic. 'I know what it feels like to be deceived, especially when everyone else seems to know what is going on and you are the last to know—'

'I'm sorry, Lewis,' Jo, unable to bear it any longer, interrupted, 'but I don't quite see why you should think that Marcus's behaviour, or him leaving St Theresa's, should have any effect on me.'

There was silence in the room as Lewis stared at her. She had switched off the television when she'd sat down, and the only sound now was the ticking of the clock, the only movement the gentle drift of the curtains.

In the end it was Lewis who broke the silence. 'Weren't you and Marcus Jacobs an item?' he said quietly.

Jo shook her head. 'No, Lewis,' she said. 'Never.'

For a moment he looked stunned. 'I thought you were,' he said slowly at last. 'That night...the Seventies night...'

'That was a one-off,' said Jo.

'But afterwards...I heard...I thought....'

'Just what did you hear, Lewis?' she said, and the bitterness in her voice was only too apparent, so apparent that he threw her yet another concerned glance.

'Did you hear the gossip?' she went on, not giving him time to say anything. 'Did you hear Marcus boasting to the others that he had scored with me, that he had won his wager with Gary Kent about getting me into bed?'

'I told you, Jo,' Lewis replied quietly, 'I don't listen to gossip. I only knew that you'd gone out with him that night and I suppose, afterwards, I picked up enough vibes to think there was something between the two of you.'

'I can assure you,' said Jo tightly, 'if Marcus Jacobs was the last man on earth there wouldn't be anything between the two of us.'

'But you did go out with him that night?'

'Yes, and that was enough. Luckily, Pru was around and came to my rescue. She, too, had been a victim of his advances in the past and recognised the signs.'

'I thought Pru only brought you home because Jacobs had been drinking. So what did he do?' Lewis's voice had a sudden, dangerous edge to it which Jo had never heard before.

'He made a couple of advances but luckily it was only while we were on the dance floor. I dread to think what would have happened if I'd gone back to his flat with him, as he suggested. I imagine I would have had a lot more to contend with than a cup of coffee.'

'Well, thank God you didn't,' muttered Lewis.

They fell silent for a moment as Lewis seemed to digest the fact that Jo wasn't involved with Marcus Jacobs, as he had imagined. Then, as if another thought had just struck him, he looked curiously at her.

'Tell me,' he said, 'what's all this about Della Latham?'

Jo hesitated, but only for a moment. After all, what did she now have to lose? It had been kind of Lewis to come to see how she was feeling, after supposedly being betrayed by Marcus, but nothing else had changed.

'I know that Della Latham is your ex-fiancée,' she said at last.

'Did she tell you that?' asked Lewis. He looked surprised.

'No.' Jo shook her head. 'She merely told me that the two of you went back a long way.'

'So how did you know?' He frowned.

'Rebecca told me.'

'Ah.' He paused. 'What else did Rebecca tell you?'

'That Della had phoned you, that she wanted to see you again.'

'Anything else?'

'That you had probably met her for a drink.'

'And did my sister offer any theories on what might have come of this?' There was a tightening of the muscles around his mouth, the ensuing expression decidedly wry.

'She may have done,' said Jo guardedly. The last thing she wanted was to get Rebecca into any sort of trouble with Lewis.

He, however, seemed to have other ideas. In fact, he seemed to be enjoying himself now, sitting further back in his corner of the sofa, crossing his legs and making himself more comfortable. 'So, tell me,' he went on, 'I'm intrigued. Just what were these theories?'

'I'm not sure that I should—'

'Oh, come on, Jo, you can't leave it there,' he protested. 'I want to know. What exactly did Becky think about me meeting Della again?'

'Well, if you must know, she wasn't happy about it,' retorted Jo, stung at last into making a response. 'She was only too aware of how much Della had hurt you in the past. She said Della was trouble, and I guess she was afraid the same thing was about to happen again, especially in view of the fact that Della is a free woman once more.'

'Isn't it strange?' murmured Lewis, raising one eyebrow. 'Becky obviously doesn't know me as well as I thought she did.'

'What do you mean?' Jo flung him a sharp, curious glance.

'Well, I would have thought that Becky knew me well enough to know that I would never put myself into a situation twice which could bring about such devastating consequences.'

The implication of his words didn't for one moment sink in and Jo simply continued to stare at him as he carried on talking.

'I did meet Della,' he went on. 'Partly, I suppose, because I was curious to see what power she had held over me. I was left wondering after the first five minutes, and by the end of the evening I was wondering what on earth it was I had ever seen in her. I ended up silently thanking my one-time friend John Richards for breaking up the relationship when he did and saving me from an even worse fate.'

'And Della?' said Jo faintly, wondering if she was

hearing correctly. 'Was she hoping to resume anything?'

'At first, I think that was exactly what she had in mind,' said Lewis thoughtfully. 'But after a while I think she also saw how utterly incompatible we really were. I'm a family type of guy, Jo. Della always loved bright lights and the high lifestyle.'

'Maybe we should introduce her to Marcus Jacobs,' said Jo, and as she said it she realised that with the sense of awareness which was steadily growing her voice sounded shaky.

'Now, there's a thought,' said Lewis. 'I think they could probably be quite good for each other.'

He paused for a long moment and allowed his gaze to meet hers. 'Is there a chance, Jo, do you think,' he said softly at last, 'that you and I could be good for each other?'

'Oh, Lew.' Jo sighed. Reaching out and taking his hand, she moved closer to him and as his strong fingers curled around hers she said, 'If only you knew.'

'Try telling me,' he said, and his voice suddenly sounded husky. 'But one thing first…'

'Ycs?' she said.

'Please, don't call me Lew.'

'No?'

'Everyone calls me Lew. You're different. You're special. I want you always to call me Lewis because I just love the way you say it.'

With that he took her face between his hands, his

thumbs beneath her chin tilting it upwards so that he could look into her eyes. 'Promise me?' he said, his voice husky. 'Promise me you'll always call me Lewis?' Giving her no chance to reply, he covered her mouth with his own.

Last time his kiss had been so light she still sometimes wondered if she had imagined it. There was no such confusion this time. This time his kiss was both firm and thorough, stirring passion and a desire in Jo that left her in no doubt that his hopes for the future perfectly matched her own.

At last, but just momentarily, he drew back slightly and looked at her again. 'Well?' he said softly.

'I promise,' she whispered, 'but on one condition.'

'Which is?' he raised his eyebrows.

'That you tell me what you meant when I answered the door and you said you'd come here because you couldn't stand it any longer. What couldn't you stand?'

'The thought of you and Jacobs together,' he said. 'I put up with it as long as I could but, quite simply, I'd reached the stage where I had to do something about it. And even if you weren't prepared to change your mind about him, at least you'd know how I felt about you.'

'And now I do know,' whispered Jo.

'And just in case you are still in any doubt...' He

drew her into his arms again, silencing her with another kiss.

For the next few weeks they took things very slowly, giving themselves time to get to know each other. They went out together—to the theatre, the cinema, to restaurants and pubs. They walked for miles—on the common and once on the beach, after driving down to Sussex for the day—and all the time they talked, endlessly they talked, filling in the gaps in each other's lives and backgrounds.

They went to see the Cunningham family and somehow there was no surprise from anyone that they were together, and from then on it seemed to be taken for granted that when they did visit it would be together.

Lewis was the first to know when, following an interview, Jo was offered the job on Paediatrics.

'I'm not even sure that I want it now.' She pulled a face. 'Everything has changed. I think I'd rather stay on the day unit and be close to you.'

'Actually,' said Lewis solemnly, 'I think it's a very good job you are moving.'

'Oh?' She sounded hurt. 'And why is that?'

'Because you are a definite threat to my concentration, that's why. One of these days I shall be so busy watching you I'll give someone a little more anaesthetic than they require. Honestly, Jo, I think from the very first moment I looked up and saw your lovely eyes over the top of your mask you had me captivated.'

'So are you saying you didn't really need help with the children?' she demanded. 'That all that was simply a ploy?'

'Of course not.' He laughed. 'That was just me getting lucky for once. A genuine opportunity that arose...'

'OK, so, if you're saying you felt like that all along, why didn't you say something before?' demanded Jo. 'All those times we were together at Chilterns?'

'There was no way I was going to take advantage of that situation,' he protested. 'I'm quite old-fashioned really. I was virtually your employer and in a position of trust, and there was enough gossip going on as it was about us cohabitating, without me adding to it.'

'Oh, so you *were* aware of the gossip?' Jo raised her eyebrows.

'Let's just say I was aware of a few winks and nudges,' he replied with a grin. 'But I suppose it was when I first saw you in that dress that I realised how I really felt about you. And seeing you with the children, Jo. You were so caring...so tender... But by then,' he went on, growing serious again, 'of course, I really did think you and Jacobs had something going.'

'I thought you seemed cool towards me,' said Jo with a little pout.

'I couldn't trust myself to be anything else,' he replied with a laugh. He paused. 'But getting back to the job situation—this is a marvellous opportunity for you on Paediatrics. You adore kids and it's a definite career boost.'

'He's right, of course,' Jo told Pru later, 'but I will miss the day unit.'

'And we'll miss you,' said Pru with a sigh. 'Mind you, I was right about one thing. I always did say he was a hunk, didn't I?'

'Yes, Pru, you did.' Jo looked at her friend and narrowed her eyes. 'And while we're on that subject, what's all this I hear about you and Gary Kent?'

'Oh, that.' Pru waved a dismissive hand but Jo noticed her cheeks had grown quite pink at the mention of the ODA.

'Well, I only hope he's mended his ways,' said Jo firmly. 'I don't want my friend being messed around again by anyone.'

'Actually,' said Pru, growing serious, 'I think the episode with Marcus may have taught Gary—and a few others come to that—a lesson. Marcus was a bad influence and now that he's gone…' She shrugged. 'Gary is still a bit of a lad, but basically, deep down, he's all right.'

'Well, I'm glad,' said Jo.

'But what about you and Mr Gregson? A consultant anaesthetist no less,' said Pru admiringly. 'Can I take it from your look of radiance these days that it's serious?'

'Oh, yes,' said Jo happily. 'It's serious all right. I don't think I've ever been happier in my life.' She hesitated. 'I was worried, you know, at first.'

'Worried?' asked Pru gently.

'Yes, after Simon. He hurt me so badly…and then there was Marcus…and, well, I was afraid…'

'You were afraid you might have become frigid— is that it?'

'Something like that, yes,' Jo admitted.

'And you're not?'

'Oh, no. Definitely not.' She flushed. 'Not with Lewis. He's just wonderful, you see…'

'I'm glad to hear it.' Pru threw her a quick, speculative glance. 'We're not by any chance talking wedding bells here, are we?'

'Well, it's funny you should say that,' said Jo with a smile.

'Mummy!' shrieked Francesca. 'It's Uncle Lew!'

'Is Jo with him?' called Rebecca from the kitchen.

'Of course she is,' said Francesca, her tone matter-of-fact, as if anything else would quite simply be unthinkable.

'Hello, you two.' Rebecca was laughing as she came through to the front door to greet them. 'Come on in. It's lovely to see you both. We're actually in the garden. I was just making some lemonade. You'll have some with us?'

'Only if you share these strawberries with us,' said Lewis, handing over the large punnet they had brought with them.

'Oh, wonderful!' Rebecca pushed her dark hair out of her eyes. 'The first this year. David's in the garden. He'll be pleased to see you. Go on through. I'll join you in a moment.'

David was sitting in a garden chair in the shade beneath the branches of one of the apple trees. He had Jamie on his knee and Alistair was on the swing. They all looked up as Jo and Lewis came onto the patio, with Francesca dancing beside them.

'Look who was at the door,' she cried. '*And* they brought strawberries.'

'That must be the ultimate passport,' said David. He was still unbearably thin and somewhat gaunt-looking but he was definitely on the mend.

'Really,' said Lewis, 'I guess it should have been champagne but the off-licence was shut.'

There was silence for a moment in the garden then as his words sank in a sudden shriek from Rebecca who had just stepped through the patio doors made them all jump.

'You mean…?' she cried. 'Lew…? Jo…?'

Lewis smiled as he lowered himself into a cane chair beside his brother-in-law. 'Yes,' he said. 'I guess I must be the luckiest man alive but, yes, it's true.'

'What's true?' demanded Alistair, jumping from the swing and joining the group on the patio. He looked from one to another of the adults.

'We're going to be married,' said Jo softly, the radiance shining through her eyes.

'Good,' said Alistair.

'Francesca?' Rebecca turned to the little girl, who had sat down on the grass and was playing with her Barbie doll. 'Did you hear? Uncle Lew and Jo are going to be married.'

'I know,' said Francesca, without even looking up. 'I knew ages ago. I drew a picture of them getting married...'

And really, Jo thought as she settled back in her chair and lifted her face to the sun, closing her eyes as she did so, she, too, had known. Had always known that Lewis was the man with whom she wanted to spend the rest of her life, had known from the moment her eyes had met his over the tops of their masks—just as she had known during those special unique, intimate moments in the deep of the night when they had answered the needs of the children.

'It's been a wonderful day, Mrs Gregson.'

'Yes, Mr Gregson, it has.' Jo half turned from the balcony of their hotel bedroom as Lewis put his arms around her and held her closely against him. There was hardly a breeze to ripple the quiet waters of the loch before them, while ahead the mountains merged mistily into the twilight.

'I'll never forget that moment as long as I live,' said Lewis. 'When I turned and saw you for the first time, walking up the aisle towards me. It just took my breath away.'

'And then Francesca peeped round my dress and said "Hello, Uncle Lew, I'm here too…"'

They both dissolved into laughter, eventually growing still and silent as they continued to watch the dusk descend and enfold the landscape like a soft mantle.

'I love you, Jo,' he murmured at last against her hair.

'I love you too.' Turning, she slipped her arms around his neck while he drew her close against him, his mouth seeking hers.

The kiss was long, deep and passionate, the promise of what was to come deep and exciting, stirring emotions and desire, sharpening senses and shaping undreamed-of expectations. Until at last he disentangled her arms from his neck, drawing her away from the balcony and back into the bedroom where he closed the doors, shutting out the world.

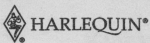

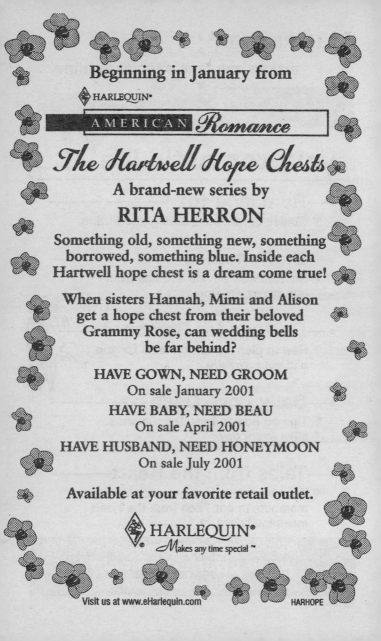

INDULGE IN A QUIET MOMENT
WITH HARLEQUIN

Get a FREE
Quiet Moments Bath Spa

with just two proofs of purchase from
any of our four special collector's editions in May.

Harlequin® is sure to make your time special this Mother's Day
with four special collector's editions featuring a short story
PLUS a complete novel packaged together in one volume!

Collection #1 Intrigue abounds in a collection featuring *New York Times* bestselling author Barbara Delinsky and Kelsey Roberts.

Collection #2 Relationships? Weddings? Children? = *New York Times* bestselling author Debbie Macomber and Tara Taylor Quinn at their best!

Collection #3 Escape to the past with *New York Times* bestselling author Heather Graham and Gayle Wilson.

Collection #4 Go West! With *New York Times* bestselling author Joan Johnston and Vicki Lewis Thompson!

Plus Special Consumer Campaign!
Each of these four collector's editions will feature a
"FREE QUIET MOMENTS BATH SPA" offer.
See inside book in May for details.

Only from

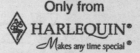

HARLEQUIN®
Makes any time special ®

Don't miss out! Look for this exciting promotion on sale in May 2001,
at your favorite retail outlet.

Visit us at www.eHarlequin.com   PHNCP01